LOST
FOR YOU

For those that love so hard they burn

Her skin tight clothes on his bedroom floor
Hands all over, starting to explore
Eyes full of lust, bodies craving more
This is everything she's waited for

I wish she knew that he wasn't right
Maybe she just doesn't

care
ton
i
g
h
t

PART ONE

Dear diary,

Ash broke up with me.

It happened a while ago now but it still feels painfully fresh. Zoe keeps saying that I'll have to crack on eventually. I guess I will soon but I'm not ready yet.

I literally feel sick just thinking about it all and he's probably not even bothered. I bet he's with her right now, cuddling close like we used to...

As you can tell, I still think about him all the time. Some of it is bad stuff, reminding me of how much I made him hate me. I must have done a lot to make him cheat on me.

But it's mostly the good times.

He was so good to me...

And I ruined everything.

I just hope that he will realise how sorry I am because I've never been more sorry for anything else before in my entire life. Losing him is my biggest regret and I feel like there's nothing I can do to get him back.

Why do I have to be such a horrible person? Why do I mess everything up? Why did I ever think that someone could love me?

But I love you, Ash. I will always love you. You were the best thing that ever happened to me and I miss you so much.

Harper

One

"It's just what people do in relationships," he says, his face contorting into a horrifying grin. His fingers trace the side of my tummy, soft and gentle. But I feel every inch in fear, waiting for it to come, waiting for it to hurt. "Don't you want to be normal, Harper?"

"Yes," I whisper back, my eyes staring into the darkness of the room. He never likes to have the lights on; he says it isn't as romantic. And I agree.

"And don't you want me?" He doesn't even let me my answer before pressing his lips firmly against mine and I have no choice but to kiss him back, to lean into it. "I thought as much." I can feel his nails sink further in, so deep that I know I'll have to live with the marks again. I'll have to plan every outfit so that I can make sure I can cover it up. All I can do is imagine everyone's faces if they could see what we are doing; it would be like they had been there in the moment, surviving through it with me.

He gets bored of that area and his hand strokes lower, teasing at the hemline of my dress as though the thought of him being there doesn't make me sick to my stomach. As though he can't see how uncomfortable I am. But then again, I'm not saying *anything, am I? I'm not asking if we can stop. I'm not telling him that I'm too tired or asking if we could just wait a bit longer.*

It's my first time; I've always had this thought that it would be special, meaningful. Ash has never been much of a romantic, apart from in those first few weeks, but I expected more than this. More than a spontaneous moment in his friend's bedroom, with the whirring of the party downstairs. This doesn't feel right at all.

"I can't," I let out. "I'm sorry, but I can't."

I feel him pull away from me slightly. I can't see his face but I can make out the whites in his eyes and he doesn't look impressed. Of course he doesn't, I've just ruined the moment that he's been looking forward to since he met me.

"I'm sorry," I say again.

"You're sorry?" he says. There's disbelief painted all over his words. "Have you just been leading me on this entire time?"

"What? No, of course not!" I say, jumping in to defend my feelings. "I like you, Ash."

"But you don't love me?" he questions, pulling his body away from me and sitting on the edge of the bed. I lift my body up but hesitate to move closer to him.

"It's only been a few weeks," I mumble.

"That's plenty of time, Harper," he says, his voice rising. But he knows he can't shout here; people will hear. He takes a deep breath and continues: "I told

you I loved you ages ago now and you still haven't said it back."

"And that's really lovely of you," I reply, placing my hand on his. I need to show him how much he means to me. I need to make him understand. "But I'm just not ready yet. I've never said those words before."

"You're eighteen," he spits. "You're not a baby." I don't know how to respond to that so I say nothing at all. Luckily, Ash doesn't mind talking. "Besides, you made it seem like you wanted this. You've been teasing me for weeks."

"I haven't!" I say. I think back as hard as I can on how I've behaved these last few weeks, wondering if I've maybe done something by accident. But those kinds of things haven't even been on my mind at all!

"Oh yeah? What about all those tiny little outfits you wear? You're practically shouting to the world 'Hey, I'm a hoe', aren't you?" he points out. My outfits aren't scandalous by any means, but I suppose my skin is on show. Maybe that's what he means. "And you asked to watch Dirty Dancing *like a million times; I know you just wanted me to watch that scene with you."*

"I just like the film," I say quietly.

"Whatever," he says, picking his shirt up of the floor. He marches over to the other side of the room and flicks the light on, highlighting the anger on his face. It's somehow worse now that I can see it properly; see the pain that I've caused him.

13

"Ash, are we okay?" I ask, fiddling with the bottom of my dress where his fingers had been only a few minutes ago. I can barely look at him without my lip quivering.

"I don't know," he says dryly. "I feel like you've lied to me. I thought you wanted this."

"I do." I don't know why I say it without thinking it through, but it just falls out and then it's impossible to take back. Surely that means I do actually want this, want him? So I do the only thing I can do: I play along to make him happy. "I do want this." Maybe if I keep saying it, I might start to believe it more too.

"Yeah?" he asks, a hint of hope in his eyes. I nod slowly. "Good, 'cos I really didn't want to breakup."

He flicks the light off again and dumps his shirt back on the floor. He's heading straight towards me... then he's grabbing the back of my hair tightly, kissing my lips with so much passion that I can barely breathe. But he's happy and he wants me and that's all that matters.

***

"You good, Harper?" Zoe asks me.

It takes me a moment to remember where I am but as soon as I see the teal blue curtains beside me, I know that I'm safe. Zoe's bedroom has been somewhat of a haven for me since I started uni, but even more so after it all happened. I don't know what I would have done without her if she hadn't helped me through Ash leaving and that's strange to think about. I'd read once that it doesn't matter how long you have known someone for; it's who they are that really counts. And I think that Zoe is one of those people; it's only been a few months since that initial awkward weekend when we all moved into our dorms for the first time. I can still picture her sticking her head through the door to introduce herself.

I had never really had friends before her, either. People in my hometown just aren't like me; I just couldn't fit in, no matter how hard I tried.

Having Ash be interested in me felt like luck. It no longer mattered that I'd been lonely once, because at least I had one person that cared about me... who wanted to spend all his time with me.

What made it difficult though, despite this, was that my mum never approved of him. She said there was something odd about him, something that she couldn't be comfortable with. Apparently he was my "mistake to make". But it meant I didn't want to tell her anything about us; she would just ruin it because of her bias towards him.

"Yeah, sorry," I reply, taking a biscuit to try to appear as least somewhat normal. "Just trying to think about an essay title."

"It's okay if you're thinking about him," she says, offering a small smile. Her brown doe eyes are looking at me kindly, enveloping my body in a mental hug. "I'd be more surprised if you weren't; you went through a lot."

"I'm fine, I promise."

It's a lie.

"If you say so," she says and I know that she doesn't believe me. "You want to go out tonight? The others are going to a new pub later; apparently it's all the rage."

"I didn't know that pubs could be 'all the rage'," I smirk. "It's probably a bad idea to be anywhere that has an ultimate supply of alcohol, though. I don't want to go down that route if I can avoid it."

"Look, sitting in your feelings is good for a bit, but you can't do it forever," Zoe says. I know that she's right. I've barely left the flat in weeks; she's been doing all my shopping for me and I've been sending sick notes to my teachers. At this point, I don't think they actually care if I attend or not; either way, they still get paid. I'm just another little burden that they don't have to put much effort into.

But it sucks, it *really* does, because I was so excited to start uni. It's literally been years of hoping I'd get in. I'd even catch the train whenever I had some spare cash just so I could come and have another look around. I'd order a coffee and pretend I was already a student here. But now that I'm here for real, it just doesn't feel the same. I'm hoping that it's because of external factors and by that, there's only really one that could have had much of an effect: Ash.

I hate how it all leads back to him, no matter what I think about. I don't even know if he even deserves it: to be thought about, to be cared about. Because I don't think that he cared about me, no matter how many times he told me he loved me. Words are just words, and that's the harshest lesson I've ever had to learn. The only way I will know if he wants me is if he shows me, if he comes back properly.

"So, you don't think you can manage it?" Zoe prompts again. I allow myself to think about it for a moment. I haven't been out with the flat group properly yet. I'd spent my first few months as a student being attached to Ash like a bloody barnacle, and ever since then, I've barely left my bed. I probably should make an effort, especially since they've decided not to give up on me. But the pub? It feels so draining. It will be loud, people will be drinking. It just doesn't sound like somewhere I should be right now.

"I'll try," is what comes out of my little people-pleaser mouth.

"Oh really?" Zoe says excitedly. She could at least try to pretend that she isn't shocked. "It's gonna be great, I promise! You don't have to drink if you don't want to and we can all -"

But I'm not fully listening anymore; I've already zoned out and I'm starting to worry about what I'm getting myself into. The only good thing about it is that there is no chance of bumping into Ash there. He's still back in our hometown, probably spending all his time with someone new... doing all the same things he did with me.

I can't believe I fell for it, thinking he wanted *me*. How stupid can I be? He's too difficult to please; there wasn't even a chance of me being worthy. And no matter how badly I want to be loved by him, I'll never be good enough.

But now I'm living in the aftermath and it's the worst place to call home.

"Wait, we should actually start getting ready," Zoe says decidedly. "What are we going to wear? You have to put on something hot; who knows who we will see tonight?"

"I'm not interested in finding anyone new," I say half-heartedly. The idea of it makes me just as nauseous as I am when I'm thinking about Ash. And that happens a lot; how am I supposed to forget about him? Other than the fact that I love him with every morsel of my being, he's also one of the hottest guys I've ever met. He's got the perfect amount of muscles, making his stomach just soft enough to be comfortable. Falling asleep on him was heaven, I swear. And then there are his eyes... piercing and blue, staring at you in a way that makes you feel like you're the only girl he will ever want.

What a lie.

"You don't have to fall head over heels and stumble straight into a relationship, Harper," she says, distracting me momentarily from my thoughts. There's no way I can half-arse my way through this part of

18

the conversation; she wants me to listen and she's going to make sure I do. "You're allowed to be happy. You deserve it!"

"I know," I say, though I don't mean it. Why should I be happy? I'm so awful that I made him hate me; I turned him into a monster. He was so lovely, so sweet, and now look at what's left. Look at what I *did*.

"But you don't," she calls me out. "Come on, let me do your makeup? Try to have a bit of fun, yeah?"

"Go on then," I say. "But please do not give me a smoky eye; I look like I've been in a fight."

"You're never gonna let that go, are you?" she laughs. I think back to the first (and only) party I ever went to last term. I've never been any good at makeup; I can't seem to blend everything properly and don't even get me started on eyeliner. So, Zoe said she would help me out and, even though she had a blast dotting the black around my eyelids, I looked positively terrifying. Definitely not like myself.

"Rightly so!"

And for a moment, a little bit of the Harper that I was before him comes to the surface.

Two

Getting ready to go out with the flat turns out to be better than I expected. In fact, I'm even grateful for the distraction and I have to admit that Zoe was right; I really need to start listening to that girl.

Luckily, she respects my eye shadow choice and she goes for something a little more neutral, which for her is really hard. Even though she is studying English Literature (we're literally in all the same classes, it's amazing), she really would rather be a makeup artist. She's just worried it won't 'secure her future' and she'd feel safer having a backup plan. I don't think choosing English was the best course for that, though.

"A degree opens more doors," she always says. She literally uses it as motivation to get through assignments, but honestly, I can appreciate the dedication.

I don't have a lot of that anymore. But I used to. Back when I was doing my A-Levels, I revised for hours every day, making sure that I knew all the content like the back of my hand. Though, I've never really understood that phrase; I can't actually picture my hand that clearly at all, but I suppose we're creatures of habit and things like that stick.

Like Ash.

Ash sticks in my mind like he's physically glued there. And I'm not even trying to prise away those memories because there are good ones in there too, ones I don't really want to forget. I still look through the photos when I'm by myself. When it's all quiet and dark outside and I feel more alone than ever. But there he is, a bundle of pixels on my screen staring back at me. And that's all I have.

"You're going to be turning away men tonight looking like this," Zoe says, putting the lipstick back in the bag. "Go look in the mirror! Tell me what you think!" She looks so happy in the moment that I decide I'll feign excitement whether I like it or not. However, I don't have to lie at all.

I look at my reflection, noticing how smooth she has applied the foundation, how the slight hint of blue eye shadow makes my eyes pop. My faded bleached hair even looks somewhat okay for the first time in forever now that it has been curled.

I look almost beautiful again; I haven't even been presentable for weeks so this feels insane.

"Wow," I say, more to myself than to Zoe, but she uses it as an excuse to come stand beside me.

"See," she begins. "Look at what he's missing out on."

But he's not the one missing out on anything; I'm the one who wasn't good enough. It doesn't matter how much I want to be angry at him; I'm the one who's to blame for anything bad he ever did.

"Come on then, the others will be ready by now too," Zoe says. "Go get a jacket and your purse."

I do as she says, almost as though I don't really process what she has said. And it's only when my fingers meet the leather of my jacket that I remember the time I had bought it.

***

"It looks so sexy," Ash says, looking me up and down after I put the jacket on. I've been searching for another leather one ever since my old one started peeling a while back, but I'm always so picky with the clothes that I buy. I'm so skinny yet tall that I feel like anything even slightly baggy will make it look like I'm a sack of potatoes. But this one feels different, like it's hugging me just right.

I stare at it in the mirror but my eyes rise to see Ash's reaction. I'm surprised to see him looking at his phone; he's taking a picture of me.

"Oh my gosh, Ash!" I say, covering my face immediately. "I look awful, please don't!" But I don't really look that bad. I don't even know why I say it.

"Shush you, you're stunning," he says, taking a look at the picture. "There's my new wallpaper."

"You're impossible," I say, taking the jacket off.

"Woah, you only just put it on!" he says, tucking his phone back in his pocket. "Keep it on."

"I only wanted to quickly try it on," I say. "I will buy it though, if that makes you feel any better?"

23

"Hmm, partly," he says. "But do you know what will make me feel much *better?" He comes closer to me, cradling me in his arms, and my brain runs a hundred miles a minute thinking of all the crude things he could say. "Let's buy something else for you to wear for me; I've got something special planned for Friday night."*

Friday night: the day of the party. Ethan has invited us all, though I think he only asked me *because I'm his best friend's girlfriend. But I couldn't say no, even though parties are most certainly not my scene. My idea of the perfect evening is snuggling up with a candle and a book. Ash hasn't read a book since GCSE English, and even then he apparently didn't read them properly. It was one of his favourite things to brag about when we first started talking and I told him about how much I love to read. Somehow I found it cute.*

But what was this 'something special' he had planned? What exactly could we do at someone's party that would be meaningful?

***

I clasp it in my fingers, doubting for a second whether I should even wear it. I bought it two months ago and I only wore it a handful of times before it became tainted with the memory of Ash. But leather jackets were always *my* thing; he just happened to be there when I bought this one. That doesn't mean I owe him anything. It doesn't mean I should text him.

But I want to so badly.

I switch my phone off completely; I can't fall into that trap. At least not yet.

"You ready?" I say, standing in Zoe's doorway. She's put on a similar jacket to my own, reminding me of how much we have in common.

"Yep!" she turns her bedroom light off and we link arms, heading outside to wait for the others.

***

The night air is cold but it's no surprise. February is usually like this but wearing such a small jacket is always worth the brief pain of trying to survive the temperature. But as soon as we enter the pub, I feel the warmth that comes with a crowd of people and I know it won't be long until the jacket comes off entirely. I don't want to think about taking clothes off though, not here, not now. Not with Ash.

"Let's sit over there!" Kelsey says. "There's a booth free!" She practically runs to it, making sure that we can bagsy it. It's lucky she does because only a second after, a crowd of disappointed faces grumbles and continues their search.

I slide into the seat next to Zoe, with Kelsey and Megan in front of us. It's cosy for a pub, at least in my experience. There are fairy lights highlighting the lining of the walls, and decorative ones in tiny glass jars on spare surfaces. There are even plants dotted about and from what I can tell, they look surprisingly real. But what I really notice is the lack of men here. About 95% of the people are young women, probably all from our uni, and I don't know why that shocks me so much. But I like it.

"You looking for someone?" Kelsey asks, her ginger hair reflecting all the lights.

"No, just checking it out," I say, which is kind of half true.

"Well, let us know if you need some wing women!" she laughs. "Right, I'll go get the first round; what do we all want?" We all tell Kelsey our orders; I decide to have a little bit of alcohol, just for the first round. I'm hoping it will help me to feel more comfortable, more like myself without all these other wasteful thoughts in my head.

She comes back sooner than expected and I stare at my drink intensely. It feels highly immature to drink for this reason, but as long as I remain sensible, everything will be fine. I take a sip of it, feeling it go down my throat.

I've got this.

"So, how's everyone been this week?" Megan asks. She has always been the leader of the pack from what I've been able to tell. There is this confident air about her that makes me jealous; she doesn't need to think things through before doing something, whereas I can over-think for days.

"Ugh," Kelsey moans and bangs her head on the table.

"Dramatic much?" Megan jokes. "What on earth have we all missed that warrants such a reaction?" And to be fair, I am insanely curious to know what's happened already.

"Remember that guy I said about, the one who I sit with in my Shakespeare class?" Kelsey asks us and we all nod along. She's told us about him so much that I feel like I know him personally. "Well, he asked me earlier if I wanted to hang out tonight."

"As a date?!" Zoe explodes.

"I think so?" Kelsey says. "I can't be certain but he looked butt-hurt when I said I was out with you guys."

"Please tell us you asked for a different night?" Megan asks and we all hang on for the answer as Kelsey's face falls into a love-struck grin.

"I said he could meet us here, and bring a friend if he wanted to since you guys would be here too," she tells us.

And it hits me. I'm going to have to be around men again. It's silly, I know. 'Not all men' and all that. And I know that not everyone is the same, but they all remind me of Ash. They remind me of what people are capable of when they realise you're not good enough for them and you just don't know until it's too late. Besides, it's too soon.

This night suddenly feels like it's going to be impossible to get through and part of me hates

Kelsey for doing this to me. But she isn't thinking about me at all. In fact, her entire focus shifts to the door we had come through just minutes before.

I turn my head slowly to see what she is looking at and I see two young men entering the pub. One of them gazes out at the crowd and says something to the other, until his gaze rests on our table and they walk straight over. I hope that he had been pointing at people behind us, but I can't pretend when Kelsey slides out of the booth, draping the first guy with a hug.

"Hey!" he says with a massive smile. He's clearly smitten with her but I remember how Ash used to look at me in that same way and he didn't exactly mean it, did he? He was planning on how to leave me for weeks before he did, I just didn't see what I was doing to him.

"I'm so glad you came, Michael!" Kelsey says. "This must be Nick! It's so great to meet you!" And, in the same friendly way she pulled Michael in, she does the same to Nick. Yet, he looks uncomfortable, as though he isn't used to being around someone like Kelsey. But neither am I, not really. "Come, sit down!"

"There's not much room," Nick points out, looking at the booth. Kelsey sits back down again, and with the four of us here, the seats seem maxed out.

"Harper and I will squish up, won't we, Harps?" Zoe looks at me, smiling. I nod and shuffle a little closer to her.

"Michael, you sit with me." And he does as he's told, leaving Nick to look at me awkwardly.

Now that he's closer, I can see properly what he looks like. He has a rugby build: broad shoulders and a bit of muscle to him. There are even the beginnings of a mullet forming but it's too short to be certain yet. I can see why Kelsey likes him; he's not my type but objectively, he's good-looking for sure.

"Sorry," he says as he takes a seat next to me. While Michael has this edgy sort of look, Nick is different. He looks kind of smart and sensible but not in a nerdy way. He has a stylish haircut where it's longer on the top, flopping over a little bit. And, to say he's a first-year student, he actually has the potential to grow a full beard. His stubble is just at the point where you can tell and it's highly attractive.

Even Ash couldn't grow a proper one.

"It's okay," I say, remembering to reply. However, I really don't mean my words when our shoulders brush against each other. We're *too* close now. If I closed my eyes, he could literally be Ash. I can almost smell him, even though Nick has a completely different aftershave on. But it could so easily be Ash, right there next to me, telling me all these things that I don't really want to hear but I'll nod along anyway.

"You good?" Nick whispers to me. My head shoots in his direction, and I realise how stupid I must look. I glance back to the table but the others have already started their own conversation about how

Kelsey and Michael first started talking to each other. Nick is the only one focused on me right now.

"Yes, sorry," I say.

"You want some air?" he asks me. "I can move over, let you out?"

The idea of space sounds good, but the thought of having to stand outside in the street alone doesn't feel appealing at all. Other than the fact that I'm at a literal pub and it's dark outside, I don't feel safe anywhere anymore. It would be far too easy to picture Ash marching up to me down the street, throwing my arms back against the wall to spit in my face.

"Actually, you can't say no," he adds. "I'll take you for a breather."

I look at him in confusion, wondering how he is able to read my mind so effortlessly when he doesn't even know me. I must look like an absolute idiot right now for him to read me this well. But he scoots back out of the booth and holds out his hand. I look at it, biting my lip.

It's different to Ash's. It's softer. Calmer.

I take it.

"Where are you two going?" Megan asks and the table goes silent.

"Just outside for a minute," Nick answers. "Don't worry, we won't be long. I'll bring her back safe." And even though this man is a complete stranger, I believe him. Because Ash never sounded that sincere, I just that pretended that he did.

Three

"I feel so silly," I say as the door closes behind us. I rest against the brick wall of the pub, pulling my jacket around me tightly to hide from the breeze a little. Nick stands a bit in front of me, close enough that it's obvious we are here together but far enough that I'm not uncomfortable. But the whole situation feels a little weird.

"You looked like you were about to have a panic attack," he says blankly, as though it's completely normal. But I don't talk to anyone about mine; they've been happening for so many years and I just never told anyone to begin with. So, the longer they went on, the harder it felt to suddenly open up. Besides, people would either think I want attention or that I'm loony, and I don't really know which is worse. "It's okay, I have them too sometimes."

"You do?" I ask, loosening a little.

"Of course," he says. "A lot of people do."

Ash didn't. In fact, mine were such a burden to him that he had to sleep with someone else; I was too much for him that he needed a release. A break from it all.

***

"Think about it a little, Harp," Ash says, cradling my cheeks and wiping the tears away with his finger. They're too wet for it to really be very helpful but I don't tell him that. I can't, can I? He's being so sweet about it all and I'm just here being a soppy mess. "You can be hard work, you know? It just gets to be a lot and I don't really know how to deal with it. But she gets it, she really does. And she helps."

"But how?" I ask. "How can sleeping with someone else help our relationship?"

"Because then I won't take anything out on you, you see?" he says. "It's healthy, I promise."

"And if I stop having panic attacks," I begin, sniffling. "Then you'll stop seeing her?" He removes his finger and shuffles back on the bed. "What? Would you? Would you stop?"

"It's not that simple," he says.

"Why isn't it?" I ask. "I don't understand. Please explain it to me." I'm begging now, desperate to know.

"Look, you just focus on yourself, yeah?" he says, placing his hand on my leg. "If you need to have a panic attack, then that's fine by me. But you can't expect me to put all my energy into you. It's not good for me. And you can't just stop so there's no point in thinking that way."

32

"But I'll try to!" I say, wiping away my own tears. "Look, I can be good. I can be okay!"

"You're not okay, Harper," he says. "I've got to go now, though. She's just dropped me a text saying she's free but I'll come round and see you tomorrow if you're feeling better, okay?" I nod and he kisses me forehead. "You're so lovely, baby. I'll see you tomorrow."

***

"Just get some fresh air," Nick says. "Then we can go back in and do it together."

"I don't get it," I say, looking at him in confusion. "You don't know me."

"Well, no," he says. "But that doesn't mean I shouldn't help you."

Even Ash didn't want to and why should he? He didn't sign up for all of this extra stuff; he just wanted a girlfriend. And here Nick is, five minutes into meeting me, making sure I'm okay. It's not right.

"I'm okay," I say. "We should go back inside and hang out with the others." I don't let him answer. I march right past him and open the door for myself, not stopping for a moment until I'm sat back down next to Zoe.

"You missed it, Harper!" she says, gripping my arm excitedly. Nick slides in beside me, silent and avoiding my gaze. "Kelsey just laughed so hard at

Michael's joke that her vodka sprayed out of her nose!"

The table erupts into laughter all over again and I join in a little. I suppose it is funny.

"That's so gross," I say lightly. *"You're* gross, Kelsey."

"You love me really!" she laughs. "What a waste of vodka though!"

"I'll get you another," Michael says. "Join me at the bar?"

"Why, yes!" Kelsey smiles, taking his hand as he leads her away.

"Right, down to business," Megan says very seriously once they are out of earshot. We all lean in a little closer. Even in just my few interactions with her, I know exactly how she can be and whatever comes out of her mouth next is going to be important and juicy. "What do we think of Michael? And Nick dear, you'll be biased so zip your mouth!" she adds, dropping a flirty smile at the end.

"I like him," Zoe says. "He seems really sweet."

"Harper?" Megan looks to me, content with Zoe's answer.

"Yeah, he seems cool."

"I don't like him," Megan blurts out.

"What? Why!" Zoe asks for the both of us. I'm pretty sure we're all surprised at her answer.

"He's already buying her a second vodka and we just got here," she begins. "He's gonna get her all tipsy so it's easier for him."

"He's not like that," Nick interrupts.

"Your lips are meant to be zipped, remember?" Megan warns playfully. "Though, I will happily shut you up another way." Nick throws his hands up in surrender and leans back in the booth, folding his arms to watch the rest of the conversation as passively as he can manage. "You know what men are like; he's just going to use her. And then, whenever he's finished, he'll dump her and move onto the next one."

I tense as she says this last bit but Zoe catches on.

"We should talk about something else," she says, trying to change the conversation. She knows exactly why it's making me uncomfortable; she's the only person I've been able to speak to about it all. Megan and Kelsey know bits and bobs, but not the ins and outs of it all. It's too hard to keep explaining, to keep reliving it.

"No, we need to make sure Kelsey is okay," Megan says. "He gives me those vibes, you know? Like he's not going to look after her properly. A bit like Ash, really."

As soon as his name falls from her lips, I can't take it anymore. I burst into an embarrassing bundle of tears, and I hate how dramatically it happens. I wanted to keep it all quiet, not show anyone how much I'm just not moving on.

"Megan, seriously!" Zoe moans. "You've taken it too far."

35

Zoe wraps her arms around me, cradling me just like he used to. But her arms feel completely different and I know I'll never be home again, because he's the only home I've had and he's with someone else now.

"Do you want to go back to the dorm?" Zoe asks me, rubbing my back. "I'm sorry; I shouldn't have pushed you to come out if you're not ready."

"We just got here," I manage to say.

"That doesn't matter," she says. "Me and you can go back; we can put a film on, order a pizza, yeah? And I'm proud of you for coming out tonight; we all are." She adds more pressure onto the last few words, and I look up to see her glaring at Megan.

"Yes, we are," Megan admits. "I'm sorry, Harper. You know me; I talk way too much."

"It's okay," I say. "Look, I'll just go back by myself. You guys have a good time."

"There's no way I'm letting you go alone," Zoe says. "Tell Kelsey where we went for us, Megs?"

"Of course," she says. Zoe and I both know she'd much rather be left alone with Nick anyway. She is already treating it like a double date with us here, who knows what she'll try once we leave.

Nick slides back out of the booth for us.

"Thanks," I whisper, because that's as much as my voice can handle. "And sorry. I'm sure Michael is great."

"Don't worry about it," he adds. "I hope you feel better."

But before I can reply, he's already sat back down and Megan has joined him on his side of the booth, threading her arms around his. She doesn't see how uncomfortable and uninterested he looks though.

"I doubt we will be seeing Megan tonight," Zoe says, clearly not noticing Nick's face of panic. "Come on you, let's go home."

***

The flat is eerily quiet when we get back. With all the lights off and the lack of sound coming from Kelsey and Megan's rooms, it feels deserted. Which, I suppose it is. Or was. But now that us two are back, I hate that it's silent. It leaves me with my thoughts to fill in the spaces and I don't want to think about all of these things. I don't want to think about the fact that Nick is the complete opposite of Ash. I don't want to think about how Ash would react if he knew I'd been alone with a boy, even though in the circumstances, there was literally nothing going on. Besides, Ash is probably making out with his new girlfriend.

"What takeout are we wanting?" Zoe says, pulling a wad of menus from the kitchen drawer. They were one of the first things we bonded over back in September. We'd all decided to order food in so we could get to know each other and when Zoe pulled these outs, we all laughed at her for how old-fashioned she seemed. That's when she admitted to being a year older than us; she'd taken a gap year to work full-time, save up a bit of money before diving back into the world of academics. From there, she basically became ancient to us and it's a joke that has yet to die.

"Pizza?" I suggest, though she knows it's coming. It's practically the only one I ever have.

"Fabulous choice," she says. "I'll go ring them up for our usual. Why don't you go get cosy and turn the projector on?"

Using the projector means we will be watching the film in Zoe's room; that's fine by me. There's no memory of Ash being in there, of us kissing on my bed that first weekend he came to visit me. There's no video calls or dates or anything. There's only Zoe and Zoe's things and… a Kitkat wrapper.

***

"Favourite chocolate, go!" I say. We're both laughing in his bed, somehow finding this game to be the most hilarious thing to exist. But at 2am, everything becomes funny. It's like our eyes suddenly have rose-tinted glasses on and we see everything differently. Brighter.

"Got to say a Kitkat," he answers. "Can't go wrong with a Kitkat."

"That's such a boring answer!" I say, whacking him with a pillow.

38

"Alright, alright," he says. "What's an acceptable answer, then?"

"Chocolate orange is the only correct one, really," I reply, sarcasm pooling from my teeth. I don't know why I say it in that tone; I mean every word of it. It's just a chocolate bar, after all. But he loves when I act like this so I keep my performance going.

"Well, it's not a bad answer, as such," he says. "But I am quite disappointed. How can you make it up to me?" As he says this last part, he pulls that look that all boys do when they are wanting to kiss; it's universal. And so I kiss him. Because what do I have to lose? This guy likes me; he's the only boy to have ever liked me in all my eighteen years. And here he is.

Wanting me.

***

It's such a stupid thing to cry over, but I can't help it. The tears begin to well up along my bottom eyelashes as I take deep breaths, throwing the wrapper in the bin where I don't have to look at it. But I know it's there, taunting me.

I force my attention away from it and flick on the projector. The light shimmers on, highlighting minute flecks of dust floating around the air that weren't as easy to see before. This is good; there's no way I can link this to Ash.

I sit myself on the bed, positioning myself on Zoe's covers so I don't wreck how neatly she's made it.

I think back to mine; I don't think I've made it in weeks. Come to think of it, I don't think I've *washed* it in weeks. Okay, I really do need to get on that... maybe tomorrow I can do a wash load.

"All ordered!" Zoe says, joining me on the bed. She has less care than me, scrunching up the covers as she makes herself comfy. "What do you feel like watching? Ooo, I know! *Dirty Dancing* is your favourite, right? I haven't seen that in ages!" I gulp before I can respond.

"It's a little tainted right now," I manage.

"Ah, no worries!" she says, not dropping the mood for a moment. It's so obvious that she's trying to be overly happy so that it's harder for me to be sad, but I'd burst out crying no matter what she was doing if I really needed to. I can do that in front of Zoe; I know there's no judgment between us. "Maybe something light-hearted? It's so random but I do have a copy of the SpongeBob Movie?"

"That's a bit different to *Dirty Dancing*," I laugh. But there's no connection to Ash, no way to connect those dots. "It sounds good."

As Zoe sets the film up, I look around at her room, trying to ground myself in the moment. Sometimes, it feels like I'm just a remnant of the past, going through the motions of each day as a corpse of who I was before.

But I'm still breathing.
I'm still here.

Four

It takes me a moment to realise that the sound of Zoe's alarm is in fact happening in the real world, not in my dream about getting Taylor Swift tickets. My eyes flutter open slowly, adjusting to the fact I'm awake and hearing Zoe's alarm… not mine. I must have fallen asleep at some point after we started the same film; I can barely remember anything past the opening credits.

"Sorry," Zoe says, shifting her body next to me. "After you fell asleep, I didn't have the heart to wake you up. You really needed the sleep".

I smile a little about how lovely that was of her. It's true; everyone knows I haven't been sleeping much and it makes me feel like such an idiot. Like, I had a breakup, a singular breakup, so why am I completely falling apart? And now everyone is tiptoeing around me, trying to help me recover from something that isn't even their fault. It's mine. It's *all* mine. Because I was a terrible girlfriend and I deserve everything I got.

"You going in for class this morning?" I ask.

"Yeah, trying to get 100% attendance this term," she says. "Not that you need to."

"It's okay, Zoe," I add, sitting up. "You should want to do that, and I should too. It's just weird, you know? Since Ash left, it feels like nothing else matters anymore. Like, my life was only important because he was in it."

"I think that's normal," she says, joining me on the edge of the bed. "You might have only been together for a few months, but it was intense. You guys were obsessed with each other, always in each other's pockets. And now that he's not there, you're gonna feel that space in your life for a while."

"How long is a while?" I ask, needing to know that it's only temporary and all of this pain has an expiry date. Because right now, it feels endless, like this *is* my life now. Forever.

"It's different for everyone," she says and it's not the answer I want to hear. "But last night was a good first step to moving on."

Moving on.

It's such a heavy phrase.

It means that Ash and I have to start going in different directions. We have to never talk again. We have to exist as strangers.

But isn't he already doing that? He'd lined up his backup girlfriend before he had even ended things with me, and they've been going strong ever since. I still have him on socials; I see all their pictures. But even if I wasn't looking, only a week after he had broken up with me, he'd made sure I knew how close they were. He'd sent me a picture of the two of them

44

in her bed, clothes off, their naked bodies were covered in the duvet. I'd stared at it for what felt like hours, analysing every detail excruciatingly as though it could somehow unsend it. Make it so it hadn't happened at all. But it stayed there on my screen and the image is still bleached into the back of my mind, living rent free.

I still don't even know who she is. I know her name and I know that she's with Ash, but that's where it ends. Her accounts are all on private (somehow I'm surprised) and I don't recognise her from home. But their paths must have crossed somehow.

"Are you going to come in too?" Zoe asks, and her face looks doubtful.

"I think I will," I decide. "I *should*."

"Really?" she says, a smile forming on her face in a motherly pride. She pulls me in for a hug before gripping my arms and looking me dead in the face. "Be ready in half an hour and we'll go in together, yeah? You're not in this alone."

"Thanks," I say, taking a deep breath.

***

As we walk up to the classroom, I notice the small crowd of students waiting about outside. The lesson before us must not have left yet, but it means that Zoe and I have to huddle awkwardly on the outskirts.

45

"There is no way," Zoe whispers to me.

"What? Why are you whispering?" I follow her gaze to look in the same direction, wondering what on earth she has seen already in the five seconds we've been here. And there he is.

Nick.

Has he always been in this class? I only went a few times in term one before I started skiving literally everything to hang out with Ash. And then the breakup happened and I wasn't going into uni anyway. But when I was with Ash, I had a habit of not really noticing anyone else; Nick and I could have sat next to each other at some point for all I knew, and I wouldn't have a clue.

But before I can think anymore, he spots us, staring right at him like a bunch of weirdos. He'd been leaning against the wall, but he pulls his body away and heads over.

"Hey," he says, as though we are friends. Which, I suppose we're not exactly *not* friends.

"Hey, how are you?" Zoe says, answering for the both of us. Words fail me. But she knows how clammy I get.

"Good," he says and then he looks down at me. I'm not even short but Nick is a few inches taller than me and I feel like an absolute midget beside him. "I hope you were okay last night."

"I was fine," I say.

46

"She was in good hands," Zoe adds, wrapping her arm around me. "What happened after we left? Anything insane?"

"Well, Kelsey and Michael had a bit too much to drink and that got a bit odd," he begins. "Megan and I had to drag them both down from the pool table before they took it too far."

"I can't believe I missed that!" Zoe spits out, then realises I am here. "Harper and I had a great night, though."

"Oh yeah, what did you get up to?" Nick asks, but he's looking at me, not Zoe.

"We watched some films on Zoe's projector," I tell him. "And we got pizza."

"Sounds like a chill night," he says. "You like pizza then?"

What kind of question even is that? Firstly, who doesn't like pizza? But, secondly, why on earth is he asking me that? It sounds like something I say when I'm nervous and losing all ability to be cool.

"Yeah," I nod.

"Cool," he says.

Zoe eyes us both. Then she smiles knowingly. "You should come next time, Nick," she says, looking like a complete mastermind. My eyes widen when I realise what she's doing but I can't do anything about it in front of him; it would be rude.

"Yeah, I'd love that!" he says, looking genuinely excited about the idea. But that's all it is: just an idea.

"What about tomorrow evening? Eight ish?" Zoe adds. Okay, so, it's no longer 'just an idea', but he's probably busy. Nick is a cool guy; surely he's got something going on.

"Perfect."

Never mind.

"Great," Zoe smiles. "We should get your number so we can send you the address. My phone is about to die though, so you'll have to put it on Harper's."

Oh, she is evil.

Nick looks at me, feeling too awkward to ask me. I slide my phone out of my pocket and unlock it, bringing it up to the 'new contact' page for him.

"Thanks," he says as he begins to type in his number. I glare at Zoe while he's distracted, but all she does is smile back and mouth: *this is a good thing! He likes you.*

I can't believe her. But when Nick passes me my phone back, our fingers brush for just a split second and it feels electric. Just like the first time Ash and I had held hands. But he's not Ash. He's Nick. And Nick might like me.

***

We are sitting on the harbour wall, watching the waves crash below us. It's July so the sea is pretty much as calm as it can be and the breeze sends my hair into an annoyingly frizzy state. But Ash is looking at me like I'm the only girl in the world. I can't even hold his gaze; it's so heavy and I'm so awkward. So I look at my feet instead, dangling over the edge above the water. One wrong move and I could easily fall in; it's scary to think about, but Ash insisted we sit on it, as though he had the perfect idea of how he wanted our first date to plan out. Almost like he'd done it before.

"I'm really glad we are doing this," he says.

"Me too," I say. We've been planning it for days now, trying to find a free moment in our schedules. We both have summer jobs and it was annoyingly difficult to try and get the same time off, but luckily I pulled a few strings.

"No, but like," he begins again. "It feels so right, you know? Like we were meant to meet. I feel like I've known you forever already." It's really sweet of him to say this. It's only been a few days and he's treating me like we've been dating for absolutely ages. I feel so lucky! "Can I hold your hand?"

I prise my fingers from beneath me, where they've been awkwardly placed when I didn't know what to do with them. He takes my hand quickly, holding it tightly in his own.

"You're mine now, Harper," he says, kissing it like gentlemen do and I can't help but blush. It took eighteen years for a boy to look at me like this, but surely it is worth it after all this time? Surely now I'll get everything I deserve, everything I've wanted?

***

49

The classroom door opens and a bundle of students start to pile out. The corridor becomes so congested that Zoe, Nick and I are as close as we had been at the pub last night, when we were squished into one side of a four-person booth. I'm glad when the throng of people disappears and we can finally find our places in the room. I follow after Zoe, taking a seat beside her, and am shocked when Nick doesn't turn away at any point. In fact, just as I'm sitting down, taking my laptop from my bag, Nick does the same right beside me. It's as though we are friends, like, *really* friends. We've hung out once, if you can even count last night, but then it hits me. Nick wasn't bee lining to sit with anyone else... maybe he was just like me. I barely know anyone other than my flatmates. And if Zoe wasn't in this class, I wouldn't even try to make friends with other people; that kind of thing is too hard.

So I accept the fact that Nick might become a part of the group, especially if anything happens between Kelsey and Michael. Besides, what harm can it do?

But I've failed the Bechdel test enough times today already, so I open up a word document and type the title for the class down: *Gender and Expectations within Austen*, one of my favourite authors. I'm in for a good class; my brain can finally focus on something other than Ash for at least an hour.

Five

My Nineteenth Century Literature class was the one that had me the most excited when I signed up for it, all those months ago. I've always been a reader, ever since I physically could be, and I think I always will be. But the classics are the books I always go back to. I can't go a single year without rereading *Emma*, reciting all my favourite lines because they've become second nature.

But since Ash left, the idea of reading has become heavy. It's a silent activity, one that lets my thoughts chaotically take over. And because of that, it's dangerous. It hurts too much.

Yet for this particular class, we are studying a book I've read so many times that it doesn't matter that I couldn't get through it again: *Northanger Abbey*. I have so many ideas and debates about it that I'm prepared enough, even though I feel like I'm going to throw up.

It seems wrong to be sitting in this room, surrounded by all these people, when I'll never see Ash again. He's just another person now. Just someone that I knew for a while, for a moment, until all connection was severed.

"Hopefully you've all read this week's text," Mr Pumas says jokingly, knowing that most of the class would rather still be in bed. "Anyone want to kick off the conversation? Get a bit of a debate going?"

I glance around the room at faces looking down at their paper and laptops, avoiding eye contact at all costs.

"Harper had this great point about allegory," Zoe says and my mouth quivers.

"Harper?" Mr Pumas prompts me. I'll get Zoe back for this later, but for now, I have to try and not look like the idiot I am.

"Uhm," I say, trying to figure out what I can say. Obviously, Zoe and I have not spoken about this text; every other word out of my mouth is 'Ash'. But she knows how much I love Austen. She's seen my collectable editions in my dorm room, kept in pristine condition on their own shelf. "Well, Catherine is an allegory for womanhood and the constant battle that comes with it."

"Could you expand?"

I take a moment to think; I'm aware of how everyone will be listening to me right now. *Nick* will be listening to me.

"At the beginning, she is unapologetically herself, having been raised outside of the confinements of the town," I begin. "But, as she begins to interact with more characters from the town, she starts to be coerced by the expectations she should have been following all along to be deemed worthy. She feels the pressure like all women do, even now. And while she comes out of it okay in the end, she still has to endure it and it's something no woman can ever really escape."

"That's great," Mr Pumas says. "Anyone want to comment on that?"

The conversation spreads throughout the room, each student slowly building the confidence to join in. And as it becomes louder, a large debate circling around, Nick leans in closer to me.

"That was pretty cool," he says, but he's not looking at me... not making it obvious that he's not paying attention to the class.

"Thanks," I whisper back. It's nice to be recognised for my intelligence, but it's nicer to be noticed for the things that I love.

***

"Couldn't we at least watch the film?" I ask Ash, clutching my copy of Emma in my hands. We're both sat in my bed, though Ash has made himself comfortable under the covers and already taken his shirt off. He's done that a lot since our first kiss; I'm actually forgetting what shirts he even owns at this point.

"It's going to be just as boring as the book, though," he moans. "Why can't you have some more interesting hobbies? Something we can both like?" I think about all the things he enjoys. He loves football,

and even though I don't really like it that much, I still go to all his games, watching him from the stands. He likes watching those trashy TV shows too, the ones with all the 'islanders' who are practically gods and goddesses prancing about in tiny outfits. I feel average in comparison; I wonder how he can want to date someone like me when there are girls who look as beautiful as that.

"I think I do," I say bravely. "I do things you like all the time."

"So it's a competition?" he says, looking at me like I've made him mad. And I probably have. He's completely valid.

"No, I'm sorry," I say. "I didn't mean it like that. What do you want to do? We can do anything you like."

"Anything?" He raises his eyebrows, sporting a cheeky grin, and I know exactly what he wants. I just don't know if I'm ready to give him that part of myself yet; I've never done that with anyone before and it's a big deal. I want it to be romantic and perfect and like it always happens in the movies.

"I don't know, Ash," I say quietly.

"Just a little bit? We don't have to go all the way?" he says and I know that I can't say no to him.

***

As the class ends, I hang by Zoe, not wanting to be by myself for a single moment. But Nick hangs about too.

"You ready?" Zoe says to us both.

"Yeah," I reply and the two of us follow her out and from the building.

"You got any more classes today, Nick? Harps and I are done for the day," Zoe asks.

"Nothing on my schedule, but I'm going to sit in on a law lecture," he answers. Who on earth goes to extra lessons? I'm one of the nerdiest people I know, and I'm barely making it to the ones I'm supposed to go to. "You can join if you like."

"I wish I could," Zoe says. "But I've got a bunch of reading to catch up on."

"Me too," I say quickly, realising what Zoe is trying to do. She needs to literally stop; I don't want to be left alone with Nick and I have a feeling that tomorrow night, she will find a mysterious excuse to cancel, leaving the two of us to watch the film by ourselves.

"Well, I guess I'll see you both tomorrow then," he says, walking away a little sadly, as though he's disappointed.

"Harper, you ass," Zoe says, elbowing me in my ribcage.

"What!" I say, but I know exactly what she's complaining about.

"Nick so likes you," she says.

"We literally met yesterday, I had a panic attack in front of him, and then had to leave early because I'm that messed up," I recite, realising how chaotic the last twenty-four hours have been.

"He obviously doesn't care," she says. "Is it because you're not over Ash?"

I look at her; somehow I'm not surprised she asked it to bluntly but I'm still shocked that she said it.

"It's only been a few weeks," I say. "I don't *want* to be over him yet."

"I've been trying not to say anything because I don't want to make it any harder for you," she says slowly, concern flooding her eyes. "But I think we need to have a proper chat about it all. Why don't we go and get a coffee? We can sit and just have a talk."

"Is this something I'm going to want to hear in a public place?" I ask, almost too nervous to hear the answer.

"You could look at in the sense that you have to remain composed which ultimately might help you out, if you really think about it," she says and I have to trust her in this, because how could I believe in my own gut after everything I've been through?

So, Zoe and I head to the nearest coffee shop. Luckily, there's one on campus and it's relatively small but super busy, so any conversation we have isn't likely to be overheard. We both place our orders and once our drinks are ready, we take them over to a table by the window.

"Brace yourself because I really cannot hold back," Zoe says and I wince.

"Okay, this is not going to be a fun conversation," I say, leaning back in the chair.

"It's not, but it's a *necessary* one," she adds and I know she's only doing this to be a caring friend; there must be something really important that I need to know. "Ash was not good for you."

The sentence comes out easily for Zoe, but it's less simple for me to take in. I sit back up straight, ready to argue, to tell her that he's actually amazing and didn't do anything wrong, but she isn't finished.

"He was actually really horrible to you," she continues. "We could all see it but there was no point saying anything because you were completely head over heels for him; you wouldn't have listened."

"No, I wouldn't have listened, because you're wrong," I say. "It was *me*. I was the one who was horrible to *him*! I was the bad guy."

"Tell me then," she says. "Tell me what you did that was so horrible."

I fall back and think, replaying the last few months in my brain in the course of a few seconds.

"You can't, can you?" she says. "Because you didn't do anything wrong, Harper."

"I - " but I can't say anything. I want to be able to, I want to be able to save Ash's name, to tell Zoe how incredible he was. How much of a perfect boyfriend he was. How I wasn't good enough.

"I was too insecure," I admit.

"That's not you being horrible," she says, placing her hand on mine. She must have noticed my eyes darting about; must have realised how much I was struggling to take it. "That's you reacting to his shitty, narcissistic behaviour."

"Ash wasn't a narcissist," I cut in.

"Harper," she says, more seriously now. "Ash would disappear for days without saying a thing, just to make you hurt. You hated that, remember? It would make you so anxious and then when you told him that, he'd turn it on you."

"I shouldn't have been so worried; he just needed space," I say.

"There is nothing wrong with how you reacted, Harper," Zoe says. "You need to realise that. He was abusive. *Emotionally* abusive. Maybe even other kinds, I don't know."

"He never hit me," I say, needing her to know that.

"That's not the only way someone can hurt you," she says, looking sad. Looking like I'm something to pity. "Ash was not a good boyfriend."

"You don't know anything, Zoe," I say. "You weren't there."

"We all watched it happen right in front of us!" she says, raising her voice. She realises quickly enough and leans in closer to me, adding more quietly: "You need to see him for what he is, Harper, or you will never be able to move on."

"I don't want to move on! Are you not listening?" I cry out. Unsure of what to do, I pick up my bag and storm from the coffee shop, not stopping until my bedroom door slams shut and I break down on the bed.

Six

I pull up Ash's phone number, looking at his face across half of my screen. I still haven't changed the photo; I haven't even considered it for a moment because it still feels like he's mine; as though it's not over and he will be back. He just doesn't realise it yet... It sounds ridiculous, but it's all I have to go on. Moving on isn't an option, no matter what Zoe says.

My finger hovers over the 'call' button, shaking rapidly as though I'm about to detonate a bomb or something. But I just can't do it, even though I feel like I'm about to throw up. So I press on the 'message' option instead, and it brings up our last conversation, the one where he broke up with me.

And before I know it, my fingers begin to type out a message.

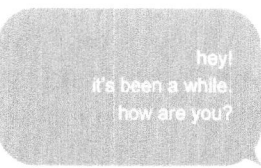

hey!
it's been a while.
how are you?

I hesitate for ages over whether or not to add a kiss on the end, but ultimately I decide not to. It won't look very cool. I throw my phone on the bed but it lands face up and, a moment later, the screen illuminates. I scramble for it, excited to read his response but it's just an email. It was silly to think he would reply so fast; no one can type that quickly… unless it was a really dry text. But I will settle for one of those if that's all I can get.

But then, unexpectedly:

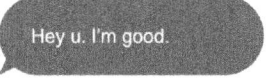

I stare blankly at the screen, shocked that he's replied so fast and unsure of how to respond. But he said "Hey U"… Hey ME. Harper me.

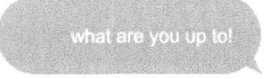

There is only one thing he can say which I don't want to hear and that is anything to do with his new girlfriend. I cannot deal with another photo of the two of them in bed together. Great, now I'm picturing it. But the tears have stopped. So has the breathing, but one step at a time.

> nothing rlly. Just chilling

He's doing nothing. He's 'just chilling'. But that doesn't mean he's by himself.

> do you want to call?

It feels risky just to ask and I don't know why I do. But I can't help myself.

After a minute, he still hasn't replied but he's read it. I can see it clear as day on my screen. But he's not started typing yet; he's probably wondering what on earth I'm thinking, asking him to call. But he replied... we were talking. It was going good!

"What was that?" Zoe asks, throwing open my door. We both look at each other. And then she looks at the phone in my hands... Ash's messages on my screen. "You did not."

"I did."

"Harper!" she complains, sitting next to me and holding out her hand for me to give her the phone. She scans over the words quickly. "You asked him to call? What were you going to say?"

"I don't know," I admit. "I just feel like if we can talk, then we can fix it."

"He doesn't want to fix it, babe," she says, stroking my back like I'm a child. "If he did, he wouldn't have cheated on you. And they're still together, Harper."

"Maybe it's because he doesn't want to be alone," I say, the tears brimming in my eyes again.

"That's not it and you know it," she says. "Deep down you *have* to know how bad he was for you. And still is! Look at you; you're falling apart over a text message. And he's probably with her right now, not giving two hoots about how you feel."

I stare at her.

"You have to start being honest with yourself," she says. And I nod slowly, understanding what she means a little bit. There's no way I can keep spending my days feeling like this; it's like someone has been pulling all of my organs from my body one by one, and then putting them back in the wrong order. And it's sickening. "You have to let him go, Harper."

Her words are heavy; there is so much meaning in them. I don't want to accept them at all. But I just ran from a coffee shop like I'm insane and the Harper before him would never have done something like that. The Harper before him did so many things differently because now I'm just a shell of who I was. And I don't want to be half of myself anymore.

"Okay," I gulp. And it takes every ounce of me to say it.

***

The rest of the day goes by in a hazy blur but it passes; it's over. And in the morning, I awake knowing it's a fresh start, even though it doesn't feel completely new. I can still taste the ache in me like it was born yesterday, but I don't want to keep crying.

I turn over to check the time on my phone and see something I really do not want to see... except, if I'm really honest, I do want it a little bit.

i don't know if that's a good idea.
abbi wouldn't like it.

Using her name hurts more than it should, but I think he knows that it would. It's like he's warning me to behave, reminding me that he didn't choose me. And I know exactly what I should do in this moment. I should delete his number and try not to think about him… but there's a little voice in my head, wondering if there's anything I can say to get him back.

I hate that I've resorted to begging, but it's nothing new. I had to do it all the time when we were

65

together; I think it makes him feel loved. Makes him feel good about himself. And I honestly don't mind doing that for him if it means he will like me again.

After two minutes, he still hasn't read it. But it's still early; I need to give him chance to reply. So, I put my phone back down and try to acclimate my eyes to the little bit of light that is creeping between the gaps in the curtains. Having already seen my phone screen, it doesn't take too long, and within a minute, I'm walking through my morning routine like a ghost.

In between each task, I go back to check my notifications, hoping that he's replied. But every time, I'm met with disappointment.

When it gets to 11am, I decide I can't keep waiting around for his response. I pack my bag and head to the library with the next essay deadline looming around me just as annoyingly as the thought of Ash does. I scan myself in and find a quiet corner to hide away in.

Ash might have left me, but I still have a degree to complete and I know I will never forgive myself if I let that slip through my fingers too.

And so I type as many words I can into the document, trying to sound intelligent whenever I bring up a new point about the representation of gender in Austen's novels. This is my thing. I know this stuff. I didn't lose it when he left; in fact, I technically have more time to dedicate to it. I can reread all of the books and maybe even add to my annotations. I can lose myself in literature like I always used to do, instead of losing myself in a boy.

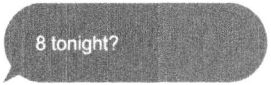

8 tonight?

My phone lights up, highlighting his message on the screen so that it's impossible to avoid. I slowly move my fingers away from the keyboard and go to reply. But eight tonight? Nick's supposed to come over to hang out with me and Zoe, or just me if Zoe decides to 'bail'.

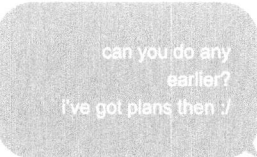

can you do any earlier? i've got plans then :/

It's hard to type. I know he won't like it. In fact, it's probably going to really annoy him and he'll start thinking that he shouldn't even be speaking to me at all.

8 or nothing

I bite my bottom lip as I read his message. There's a choice here; a crossroad. And I don't know which the best path to take is. All I've wanted for weeks is to talk to Ash about everything that happened between us, to try and make sense of what went wrong and to see if we can fix it in any way. But Nick has been lovely so far and I wouldn't just be cancelling on him. Poor Zoe has carried me through this breakup and she would tell me that this is a terrible idea. And of course, there's all the stuff she was going on about last night, about how Ash is bad for me. But I don't know if I believe all of that; I'm the one who messed up. Otherwise, he would've stayed; he would never have cheated on me.

***

A message comes through and I smile as I see his name at the top of my screen. He's been at work all day and we haven't been able to speak to each other; I've been looking forward to him finishing his shift since I woke up.

> i don't think we should
> be together anymore
>
> ...

I stare at it, hoping that it's not real. Maybe it's just a prank?

> what are you on about?

> it's not working out.

What does he mean? Yes, it's been harder since I started uni. I moved away and he stayed home and all of a sudden we were long distance. But he's not even that far away from me. It's an hour by train; we could easily see each other every weekend if he wanted to, but he never does. There's always some excuse.

> can we call at least? i don't think this should happen over text.

I don't think it should happen at all, but I'm not joining in and breaking up over message; we're not children. And, if we call, it will be easier to convince him to change his mind. We can talk about what's really bothering him and I can help him feel better.

i'm with abbi.

He's with her.

The girl who I 'shouldn't worry about because she's just a friend'.

The girl who sends him multiple kisses and quite obviously flirts with him but I'm the one who's 'feeling insecure'.

you're at her house?

I ask it, though I don't know if I want to know the answer. I watch my last message as it turns to 'read' but it isn't followed by any typing. I'm about to send another text when his little bitmoji appears as a notification. I'm not sure why he's moving the conversation elsewhere until I see that he's sent me a picture on snap. I press on it without any hesitation.

And I want to vomit.

Because yes, he is at her house. But he's also in her bed. With his arm around her. And neither of them are wearing anything.

***

70

It all comes flooding back to me: that night and everything that came before it. All the horrible times I had when he wasn't there because it became normal for him to retreat without saying a thing. All the times when I'd done nothing wrong but he would still find something to pin on me.

Zoe was right; I've been an idiot. Or at least, he's not as innocent as I've been believing. We both did wrong by each other and now is my chance to fix it all. But just as I'm about to send a reply, Zoe knocks on my door.

"You ready?" she asks and I nod. "We're gonna be late! Hurry up!"

I put my phone in the back pocket of my jeans, and grab my stuff. It's so weird how easier it is to do things just because his name is on my phone again. It's like nothing happened. There's no Abbi. Just us. Harper and Ash.

Seven

Throughout the day, I wait for a moment for Zoe to leave me by myself so that I can reply to Ash. But she never waivers for a second and as the hours tick by, I worry that I won't be able to tell him my answer at all.

We are now sat in the campus library, both of us working on our assignment. My phone is in between both of our arms, looming with so much pressure that I could literally combust. I can just imagine how annoyed Ash is becoming; he will be questioning why on earth I asked to call and then just never replied after opening the message. It's comical really: the timing of the universe.

But the day keeps going by and the sun sets, yet still, I can't find an opening. I even wait for him to double text, worried that Zoe will see and realise that I kept texting him. But when no such message comes through, it hurts; he doesn't even want to know *why* I haven't been around all day. *Why* I left him on read like he always used to do. But I suppose he doesn't need to hang onto my every message like I do his; he's got Abbi. He was at hers last night; he's probably still there now. Both of them kissing. Both of them close to each other.

"Can we head back now?" I say to Zoe, suddenly feeling sick. If Ash and I don't have this call, then he and Abbi are just going to become closer and we will never have a chance to redeem what we lost. I can't leave it to chance.

"We can," she says but I know there's a catch coming. I can see it behind her eyes; she's got a plan of some kind. "But I'm having your phone."

"What? Why?" I ask, perhaps a little too defensively.

"I'm not stupid, Harper," she practically laughs. "I've seen you eying it all day, as though you're scared it's going to grow legs and walk away. And you can't tell me it's nerves about your essay because you've barely added a single word in hours."

I look at her dumbfounded. How on earth has she been watching me enough to realise that without me noticing?

"You can't text him again," she says, this time more seriously. "You can't begin to move on until you cut contact completely."

I don't say anything.

"You already did?" she asks, but again, no words come out in reply. Instead, I sport a guilty face. "Okay, you definitely need to give me your phone. You can't ruin your date tonight for some absolute jerk."

74

"It's not a date!" I jump in as I watch Zoe slide the phone into her bag. "And Ash is not a jerk…"

"Keep telling yourself that," she says. "Hopefully one day you'll realise how blind you've been. Now, in the meantime, tonight is definitely a date."

"It can't be a date if you're there," I add. "I don't think Nick is in to that sort of thing."

"And you are?" she laughs.

"You know what I mean!"

"Look," Zoe says. "Maybe I'll stick around at the beginning, make sure everything is going okay. But then I'm leaving you two to it. Just give him a chance, yeah?"

"Why though? What about Ash?"

"Is Ash here right now?" she asks and I shake my head reluctantly. "No, but Nick is. And I think you two would be a good couple so at least indulge me; I'm begging you. If tonight goes awful, then there's no harm done. You can just be friends. But you have to start putting yourself out there again; you need to realise that Ash isn't the only boy out there. And, more importantly, you need to realise that not all men are like him."

As much as I can try and enjoy myself with Nick tonight, he won't be Ash. No one will ever be and I might have lost my one chance of getting him back.

"Now, let's head back and get you all pretty for your date!" Zoe says and we return to the flat.

***

Ash and I have never been on a date before and so I have no idea what to expect. I don't even know what he has planned but he promised me that it was something so amazing that all of my friends will be jealous. He's really set the expectations high so I'm curious if he will be able to live up to them.

So far, he's not doing great. I've been waiting at the bus stop he told me for nearly fifteen minutes… he's only ten minutes late but he hasn't even dropped me a message. I almost feel like he won't show up at all. He's probably met someone cooler than me and decided to drop me. I can't blame him for that.

But just as I'm about to send him a text and ask if everything is okay, the bus pulls up and a tired-looking Ash steps out onto the footpath, just mere meters away. He clocks me almost instantly and walks towards me and, while I have the biggest grin that embarrassingly won't go away, he looks completely chill. I don't know how he does it; I'm such a mess, as though I'm still fourteen.

"Hey," he says, pulling me in for a casual side-hug. I bask in the moment, realising that this is the first physical contact we've ever made. There's something so special about going from calling every day on the phone to seeing each other in the flesh.

"Hey, how was the ride over?" I ask, looking at the bus as it pulls away.

"Just public transport, isn't it?" he says, dryly.

"I guess," I add. "So, what's the plan?" He looks at me, as though I am talking absolute madness, but then the realisation hits.

"Oh yeah," he replies. "First stop is a coffee shop."

I smile, knowing that he's remembered my love of caffeine from when I told him the other day. It's nice to think he really listens to what I have to say; it makes me feel special. I've never had someone like that; someone I can talk to about anything and they will smile and nod along and really focus. I like it.

***

As Zoe curls my hair, I look at my reflection in the mirror, thinking about how much I've been through in just these last few months. I don't feel like myself at all. I don't even think I look the same; I'm older now, more experienced. But it's not in a good way and I can tell by the droopiness of my eyes. I reckon it's from all the crying I've done but maybe this is just what happens as you get older. Maybe life really does get harder, just from existing, and this uncomfortable feeling in the pit of my stomach is something I'm going to have to accept.

"You look beautiful," Zoe says, placing the curls around my face, cupping them softly in her fingers. I'm not sure if it does anything but my skills stop at books; hair is not my forte at all.

77

"Thanks," I say and part of me has to admit she's done a good job at brightening me up. "Are you sure I'm not overdressed, though?" I look at the outfit she's put me in and wince: a black mini skirt with tights and a knitted sweatshirt.

"Of course not," she says. "It's a nice mix of casual and hot. Besides, with your legs, you should show them off. Nick will be full on goggling as soon as he sees you!"

"What if I don't want him to goggle?" I ask.

"He's already spent half his time since he met you just thinking about you," she says.

"How do you know?" I pester.

"I just do," she replies, putting the curling wand on the heat proof mat. "Don't touch it; it's hot."

"I'm not a child, Zoe!" I say, but I laugh because her warning is totally necessary. Since being at uni, I've burnt my skin at least four different times and not just from hair-related products. I can't even make a cup of coffee without searing my skin.

My phone buzzes; I can see where Zoe has put it on her desk, positioning herself purposefully between me and it.

"I will check; you stay there," she says, warning me with her finger. Every ounce of me hopes that it is Ash asking why I haven't replied yet, but I'm sure her reaction wouldn't have included her current smile if it is him. "It's Nick! He's outside!"

"If he's outside then you need to shut up," I laugh. "He will definitely hear you from here!"

78

"Oh hush," she dotes. "He'd love to know we've been talking about him! Now, spray some of my perfume and go get him! And tell him that I had a last minute assignment I forgot about that's due tomorrow!"

"I knew you'd ditch!" I say. "Zoe Rivers, you are so damn predictable. But *please* stay."

"I can't! It's not a date if there are three of us," she says, as though I wanted this to be a date in the first place. "Look," she says, going into full pep-talk mode. "It's okay if you don't like Nick in that way, and it's okay if this date ends up being really bad. It's even okay if you think about Ash the whole way through! But it's a step you need to take. You need to promise me that you will try."

"Try what?" I ask, though I'm listening intently.

"To not close yourself off."

It's a big promise, especially because I feel like Ash is the only boy I want to be with right now, or maybe even ever. But when she points out her pinky finger at me, I grip onto it with my own.

"I promise," I say. Because I mean it. I really will try.

What's the alternative? Be sad forever?

Eight

I walk up to our front door awkwardly, hearing my footsteps like they're echoing against the walls of the hallway. My fingers are shaking as I press down on the door handle, and my heart beats quickly when I see him stood on the other side of the door.

"Good evening," he says, sounding way more gentlemanly than you'd expect a first year uni student to.

"Hi," I reply. I hold the door open to let him past, closing it softly behind him before realising he's stood there waiting to follow after me. "Zoe can't come anymore so we'll have to watch it in my room. I hope that's okay." He shifts a little, looking at his feet with his hands in his pockets.

"Of course it is," he says.

"Cool," I say. "Uhm, my room is this way." I point down the corridor, before realising I should probably just show him the way. As I guide him in, I pray silently that my room is tidy and smells nice. No matter how I'm feeling about Ash, I still want to make a good impression and I cannot for the life of me picture the state I left it in.

For so long, it's not been great. I've struggled to put things away back in their places, and I don't even remember the last time I vacuumed, but once I set my eyes on it, I realise that I must have been doing better recently. Because it's really not that bad. There's even a candle lit on my desk by my laptop (which, by the way, is set up with Netflix already on the screen). Zoe must have quickly set it up when I went to answer the door; what a sneak.

"Wow," he says, sitting down on the edge of the bed. "You didn't have to do all of this."

The way he says it makes me feel like this definitely isn't a date after all; he didn't want me to put any effort it or anything. It was just meant to be a simple hangout among friends, but Zoe isn't here and now there's a candle and it all looks like a little too much.

"I'm sorry," I say, not really sure what to do about it all. It would look weird if I suddenly blow the flame out.

"Don't be," he says. "I just wasn't expecting it, but it's nice."

It's nice?! What does that mean? Is this a date? Isn't it?

"So, what do you want to watch?" he asks, and I shift into gear, squatting down by the laptop.

"Up to you," I say, because really I'm scared to suggest anything in case I choose awfully.

"What's your favourite film?" he asks and he says it so sincerely that I turn to face him.

"My favourite film?" I say back, shocked I've been asked.

"Yeah," he says. "You've got to have one."

And I do. I *do* have a favourite film. But I think back to how Ash was about it and I feel silenced.

***

Our first date has gone so well that he's asked to come over. My parents are out at work so they will never know that I've invited a boy over. It all seems like it's okay. Like it's meant to be. And so here we are, sat in front of the TV in the living room like we're twelve again. And before us is a pile of chocolates I've been saving for a moment just like this.

"What do you want to watch?" I ask. "I've got pretty much all the streaming platforms."

"Show-off," he says with an eye-roll, and I laugh. "Any recommendations?"

"I love Dirty Dancing*, but I don't know if it will really be your thing," I admit, but I'm still excited to tell him. There's something so wonderful about how as we get to know each other more and more, we will both learn all these random things about each other that no one else knows. And this is one of the first of those facts.*

"That pile of shit?" he questions, raising an eyebrow. I can't tell if he's joking but I choose to act like he is.

"It's amazing!" I say, defending it.

83

"Ah, I know why you like it so much," he says, as though it's all clicked into place for him. "You just like those scenes." I pause, thinking about what he means. And he's completely wrong.

"What? No, I -"

"If you wanna watch that kind of thing, we might as well watch the real thing," he laughs.

"So, you don't want to watch it?" I ask again.

"We can watch it," he says decidedly. And I smile, knowing that I can spend the next hour and half giving him a running commentary of all my favourite parts and swooning over Baby and Johnny as they fall more in love, just like Ash and I will do. "It's just going to become background noise anyway." I'm not entirely sure what he means by that, but I put the film on and get cosy in a blanket, not caring too much about Ash's hand laid flat on my thigh.

As the film goes on, he listens along silently to everything I say. But his hand creeps higher; he holds onto my skin more tightly with every scene that goes by. And then, just as the montage to "Hungry Eyes" starts playing, his takes his fingers and thumb, twisting my head to face him.

"Yeah?" I say quietly.

"Don't say anything," he says and he kisses me. But it's not how I'm expecting. It's hard, passionate, strong, and there's no escape. So I return the energy, holding onto his arms and trying to bask in the moment that is our first kiss.

Our first kiss.

There's always so much pressure around these things, but here it is, happening in the moment. And this means that Ash really likes me.

"I love you, Harper," he says as our lips slightly pull apart.

He doesn't give me time to respond; I'm not sure I can anyway. Instead, he lunges his tongue back into my throat. We stay this way for a few minutes more until he pulls away, combing his fingers through my hair.

"You didn't say it back," he says, looking me dead in the eye. I stare back at him, unsure of how to navigate this situation. I'm not ready to 'say it back'. This is our first date, our first week of knowing each other. But he wants me to.

***

"It's *Dirty Dancing*, but I know it's a bit cringe," I say, wishing he hadn't asked me.

"I've not watched that in ages!" Nick says, sitting up in excitement. I shuffle a little bit. "We can watch that for sure! Pop it on!"

"Are you sure?" I ask again. I'm a little bit worried about how *for* this he is; it's weird.

"Of course," he says with a smile. "It's your favourite and I like it so that makes it a good choice."

"Okay, thanks," I say slowly as I begin to type in the title. It comes up and I flick it on, which makes me wonder what to do next. "Should I turn the light off?"

Ash always liked the light off; it got to a point where I didn't even need to ask, but with Nick, I can't just assume.

"You can leave it on," he says. "It's up to you though; if you prefer watching stuff in the dark, you know?"

"I guess I'll turn it off," I say, realising how much I needed things to be the same. I might not have Ash anymore, but if nothing comes from that, maybe I can try and do those same things with Nick?

"Fine by me," he says. I shuffle over to the light switch, feeling his eyes on me. I'm more comfortable now we are plunged into darkness, but it feels insanely weird when I sit next to him. At first, we're slightly too close and our knees brush against each other.

"Sorry," I say, wriggling to the side a little.

"It's okay," he whispers back. The film begins, the opening credits lighting up the room. I can barely move; I'm too worried to accidentally touch him again. I don't even say anything... I just focus fully on the characters on the screen, hoping that if Nick wants to talk, he will be the one to say something.

But by the time we're halfway through, neither of us have moved a muscle.

"I -"

"It -"

We both try to break the silence at the same time and we laugh in realisation. I brush a strand of

86

hair behind my ear, suddenly feeling even more aware of my body's existence.

"I was just going to say that I love this part."

"Me too," I reply. It's nice to know he's actually watching it, that he wants to make a comment on what's going on in the film. It doesn't feel much like a date, though. Surely he would have tried something by now? Told me that he loves me, or at least likes me? *Kissed* me?

But all we do is talk about the film, both agreeing that *Hungry Eyes* is the best song on the soundtrack and that we'd both be absolutely terrible if we were in Baby's situation. I can't dance to save my life and Nick laughs about how he has two left feet.

"You're so cliché!" I joke, hitting him softly on his arm. He looks down at where we made contact and drops a small smile.

"I could say the same about you," he says and I raise an eyebrow questioningly. "Your books." He points up at my bookshelf and I remember how many cheesy romance novels I have.

"Oh my gosh," I squirm, throwing my hands over my face in embarrassment. "I swear I read other books too."

"There's nothing wrong with them," he says, pulling my hands down with his own. He doesn't let go as he rests them on his lap and I realise how terribly close we are to one another. "You could tell me about them one time."

87

"I'd like that," I whisper. But I'm not thinking about books right now. I'm thinking about Nick and how his lips are close enough to touch mine. About how I can smell his aftershave.

About how I'm kissing him.

I don't expect it. I don't even know *why* I'm doing it. But I lean in and our lips press against one another's; it feels so right. I pull back slowly, letting the kiss exist in a small, romantic moment, and our eyes meet. It's only now that I see the soft blue around his irises as he looks at my own.

"Thank you," I say quietly. And then I cringe at myself.

"You're welcome, Gilmore," he replies, his voice deep and low.

"You've seen *Gilmore Girls*?" is what my attention turns to; I forget about the fact we've just had our first kiss for a moment.

"About four times!" he laughs.

I'm about to ask him a million questions; I need to find out which team he's on out of Dean, Jess and Logan. And then I want to find out his opinion on Luke and how incredible he and Lorelai are together.

But I can't.

Because before I can even open my mouth, I hear banging at my window... loud knocks coming from behind the curtains.

Nine

"What on earth," I mutter, practically jumping in shock. I pull my hands from Nick's and go over to the window, throwing the curtain aside. It's so dark outside now that I can't quite see what's going on, but then his face presses up against the glass.

"Open up!" Ash shouts.

I hover by the window, too shocked to move.

He's here. Ash is *here*. Outside my window. At my uni.

"Ash?" I question.

"Uhm, are you all good?" Nick says, reminding me that he's here.

"I'm *so* sorry," I stutter, turning around to look at him apologetically. "Ash is my ex. I didn't know he was…"

"Ah, I should leave," Nick says.

"No," I say, stepping from the window. But then I remember that talking to Ash has been all I've wanted for weeks. Just because I kissed Nick doesn't mean that I can't do that anymore; in fact, Ash is more important. We spent months loving each other and I don't want to give that up over someone I *just* met, even if he has been lovely the entire time.

"It's okay," he says. "We'll talk later." He hesitates by the door. "I would have given you a goodbye kiss but - " He looks in the direction of the window and grips onto the back of his neck. "I'll see you in class, Harper."

I don't exactly want him to leave but what can I do?

The only thing I can do: talk to Ash.

I take a deep breath and open the window, feeling grateful that my room is on the ground floor.

"You didn't reply to me," is his opening line.

"Zoe took my phone," I say, and I realise now that she still has it. She's probably had one ear up to our door for the last hour; maybe she will even bump into Nick in the corridor and ask how it went. And who knows what he's thinking now. I've probably ruined anything I could have had with him, but this is Ash we're talking about.

"Right," he says, as though he doesn't believe me. But he doesn't really know Zoe very well, or any of my friends for that matter. "Look, we need to talk. Can I come in?"

I glance back at my room. We have so many memories here and part of me has been feeling like we'd never make any more. But he's here, and he's asking, and I'm telling him to come to the door. I'm just praying that he won't bump into Nick because I don't even want to think about what Ash will do. Why does he have to choose now to show up?

I close the window and pull the curtain back over it, taking a deep breath as I realise what's happening. It feels almost too good to be true, as though I must be imagining it. But it becomes even more surreal as I head back down the corridor, tracing the steps I'd taken with Nick earlier this evening.

"Hi," he says, as I pull the door open. There he is. Looking just like he always did. Like nothing has changed and we haven't been apart for weeks. Like I can forget everything and we could kiss right here, right now.

"Hey," I say. "Do you want to come in?" I feel a little stupid, knowing that the whole point of me coming to let him in was to... let him in. But I'm so nervous. I swear my goose bumps have their own goose bumps and my breathing has gone all funny.

All the way back to my room, I can feel his eyes on the back of me and it makes it difficult to move properly. It's like I'm more at risk of being clumsy because he's here. But that's just what happens when you like somebody; it's normal.

I'm normal.

"It's exactly as I remember it," he says, stepping into my room and closing the door behind him, leaving the two of us completely alone and away from everybody else. All I can hope is that Zoe didn't hear us coming in; she's going to be so annoyed when she finds out he's literally here in person, let alone just texting. But I can deal with that later. For now, all I want to do is talk to Ash and fix everything.

"It's not been too long since you were last here," I say, wondering if it is the right thing to say. Truth is, I don't know how to navigate this situation at all. I'm so scared that if I put one foot wrong, the whole thing will go up in flames and we'll be in a worse position than we already are. I don't want to think about it how much more awful it can be, but I know it's possible.

"No, it hasn't," he says. He invites himself further in, sitting down in the bed after pulling his shoes off. He never takes them off properly; I don't even think he's had to tie the laces since we met. While it may be breaking his shoes, it's a stabbing reminder of a little Ash mannerism that I never forgot about and never will. "Look, it really hurt when you didn't reply earlier."

It *hurt* him? I don't even know how to respond to that. In comparison to what he's done to me, it feels like nothing. I could have just been busy and couldn't reply yet, which is kind of what did happen, even if Zoe did take my phone from me. I just had to prioritise other things for a day; I'm not at uni for the hell of it, after all.

"I've just had stuff to do," I say, shuffling to sit on the bed too. I make sure to leave some space between us. No matter what's happening right now, he still has a girlfriend back home. "Does Abbi know you're here?"

"No," he says quickly. "There's nothing to say."

I'd argue the opposite, mainly because I've been in Abbi's place before. I know how painful it is when you don't what Ash is doing and how it feels not being able to trust him. Only this time, he's not doing it to me. He's doing it to the next one. Exactly the same.

"Oh," is what comes out of my mouth.

"Look," he begins again. "*You're* the one who messaged *me*. And then you just stopped. You've gotta see how that could make feel?"

"Yeah," I say, realising how badly I've behaved. "You're right, I'm sorry. I just… I was at the library with Zoe and then -"

"And then you were on a date," he spits out, as though I've done something wrong. And I guess I have; I've basically waved a massive flag saying that I'm moving on.

"It wasn't a date," I say stubbornly. I'm still not sure what it was so it's not exactly a lie.

"You were alone in your room with a boy, with the light off, watching a film," he says, pointing at my laptop screen. "No surprise at the film choice. Is that what it is, Harper? You were missing me, missing how I touched you? You were just trying to replace that?"

"No, that's not it, Ash," I say, throwing my hands up. "Zoe was supposed to be there too."

"Then where is she?"

"I -"

"Don't lie to me, Harper," he says. By now, his face has been pulled tightly and his fists are curled on his lap. I lean back a little on the bed, remembering all the times he was like this before.

"I don't know what's wrong with me, Ash," I cry, tears bundling down my cheeks all of a sudden. I bring my hands up to my face, trying to hide them, but it's no use. Ash moves closer and puts his arms around me, kissing my head softly.

"Tell me more," he whispers.

"I just want to make you happy," I say, burrowing into his chest. "That's all I've ever wanted. But I can never get it right! Before, you were always so mad at me, I was always messing up in some way and you had to find somebody else."

I pause, wondering if he will say anything. But he doesn't.

"And now," I begin again. "I thought it was my second chance. But I'm still just as useless as I was before. I'm not enough for you, am I, Ash?"

"Shhh, it's okay," he says, rocking me back and forth a little, cradling my back. Being in his arms feels like home again and I loathe the moment I'll have to pull away.

"I'm really sorry," I blubber. "Really, really sorry."

"It's okay," Ash soothes me. "I forgive you."

It's all I've wanted to hear for weeks, so much so that as soon as it's out there in the open, I fall into his body all over again.

"Please come back," I beg. "You don't really love Abbi like you love me, do you? I miss you."

"And I miss you too, baby," he says, pulling me away to look me in the eye. "But I love Abbi too. I can't just leave her for you."

"You left *me* for *her*."

"That's not fair, Harper," he says, taking his arms away completely, leaving me by myself on the bed again. "That's different."

"Why is it?" I ask. "Why is it different?"

I look at him, desperately needing an answer. But I don't think he's capable of giving me one; I don't think he understands it himself.

"Please, Ash."

"I can't come back, Harper," he says regretfully. "You're not good for me."

"I can do better!" I plead, grabbing his hands in mine. "I can love you so much better, just give me a chance."

"I don't know…" he says, looking me in the eye again. "How do I know I can trust you?"

"You can! You can trust me, I promise!" I say. "Pinky promise!" I hold out my little finger and he looks down at it. Pinky promises were always our thing; they were unbreakable. He *has* to believe me because I don't want to keep living my life trying to move on from him, from *us*.

"You mean it?" he says.

"Yes, I mean it, Ash. I've never meant anything more," I say, trying so hard to convince him. And then... our little fingers are intertwined.

"Okay," he says quietly. "I believe you. We can see what happens, yeah?"

"So, we might get back together?" I ask, though I'm afraid to know the answer. But I have to know what he means, I have to fully understand what is going on so that I don't disappoint him again.

"Maybe," he answers. "Let's not think about that right now."

He places a hand softly on the side of my face, curling his fingers through my hair. I can feel his breath against my skin and all the times we kissed before come back to me all at once. This is what I want. Ash is what I want. And here he is, wanting me again.

"I love you, Harper," he says, just loud enough for me to hear. It's almost like he's saying it to himself, reminding him of how amazing we are together, how much we are meant to be.

"I love you too, Ash," I say back, because I know it's what he wants to hear. And he proves me right as he plunges towards me passionately, pressing his lips against mine as though it will be the last time we ever kiss again. I kiss him back, scared that if I stop for even a moment, he will pull away. But I need him close. As if on cue, he bites my bottom lip, pulling it with his teeth as his head falls back and eyes open, a small grin glistening in them. His teeth release me, and I smile back at him.

"God, I've missed you," he sighs. "Don't ever leave me again."

I don't have the heart to tell him that he's the one who left me.

We kiss a while longer, wrapped up in each other's arms. It feels so perfect, so right, and I can't think why he would ever want to leave this behind. Ash and I just work so well together, like we were made to be with each other. All I can hope is that he sees that now. He maybe just needed the time away to realise how much he loves me, and now that he's seen it, he will leave Abbi and we can go back to being Harper and Ash like none of this ever happened. That's what I want.

It's *all* I want.

"I should go back," he whispers into the darkness. I'm laying on his chest, my leg over his and my arms around his body. Back when we were together, we'd cuddle like this all the time; it was always Ash's favourite position because he had a good grip of my ass and could hold onto my hair if he wanted to. It wasn't a shock whenever it turned into sex.

"Don't go," I say, holding onto him tighter. "I like having you here."

"And I like being here," he says. "But I can't stay overnight. Mum's expecting me home and the last train will be leaving soon."

97

"Okay," I admit defeat, knowing that he has a good excuse. "Well, can you come tomorrow? You could let her know that you're staying over."

"I can't tomorrow," he says, leaving the 'why' hanging.

"The day after?"

"I'll let you know when I can see you again, okay?" he says, pulling his body from mine and heading towards the door where his shoes are. I sit up on the bed, just about able to make out his body in the dark. As though he is reading my mind, he flicks the light on but doesn't look to me. Instead, he starts to aggressively shove his feet into his trainers and puts his phone in his pocket.

I wait for him to give me a goodbye kiss, feeling like there's no way he will be able to resist after what just happened. But he grips the door handle, pressing it down and opening the door.

"See you soon," he says. But he's still not looking at me.

Ten

After he leaves, I tiptoe over to the window and pull the curtain aside just enough to peek out. I want to watch him as he leaves, just to remind myself that he was here, and maybe see if he looks back.

I spot him quickly enough, walking up the path away from my block, pulling his phone to his ear. He's most likely letting his mum know he's on his way home so she doesn't worry; he's so lovely. And he might be mine again.

The waiting around is going to kill me though. All I'm going to be able to think about from now until the next time we talk is what will happen between us. We spent about half an hour just making out tonight; that's got to mean something. He didn't even want to have sex, which, for Ash, is rare. It actually felt good, like he was respecting me and the fact that we have been apart. Maybe he was even respecting Abbi, not wanting to go further until he breaks it off with her.

Either way, it's all coming together again. All I have to do now is convince Zoe to like him and somehow let Nick down gently. I should definitely apologise too for how quickly tonight ended. And for *why* it ended like it did; I'm sure he will understand when I tell him how much Ash and I love each other.

Oh my gosh!

Ash and I love each other. We're practically together again!

Getting ready for bed has never been easier. I smile the whole way through, excited to check my phone for a goodnight message from Ash, but when I finally climb into bed and power on my phone, his name isn't there. But Nick's is:

> hey, i just wanted to say i had a good time tonight.

> i hope everything was okay after i left and that you have a lovely sleep!

Guilt tiptoes through me. It's such a sweet message and he sent it ages ago. He's probably waiting for me to reply before he can go to bed; that's how I am with Ash. But what can I say? *'Me too but Ash and I are getting back together and we made out in the same spot you and I had our first kiss literally hours before?'* No, this needs to be something

I tell him in person. But leaving him on read isn't something I can do either.

me too! see you in class :)

I play it safe, avoiding anything that Ash might see as cheating. But when the 'read' receipt creeps onto the screen before I can even minimise our chat, I feel like someone has punched me in the stomach. It's even worse when the three little dots show up at the bottom and then disappear only a second later.

Ash is right. I *am* an awful person.

***

I wake up with a horrible headache. Thinking about last night made it difficult to get much sleep and I groan when I realise that I'm supposed to be going to the library with Zoe again to work on our essays. I need to stop agreeing to things in advance: the introverted part of me cannot deal with it.

So I check the time to see how long I have to get ready. It's only 8:30, giving me around half an hour to make myself look somewhat presentable.

Actually, I need to look drop dead gorgeous because Ash has finally sent a message!

GM xxx

There's not much to it; it's short and he hasn't even used full words. But there's three kisses at the end and that's all I need to know that he still loves me and wants me. It proves that I didn't just imagine what happened last night.

good morning handsome! <33333

It might be a bit too much but I just can't help it when it comes to Ash; I have so much love for him that it just spills out of me. He's used to it by now; he probably loves how much attention I give him. And that works for me because I love giving it.

But there's another message too and it's from Nick. This one makes me feel nauseous, though.

Zoe invited me to the library with you guys. I hope that's okay x

First of all, Zoe does not even have Nick's number so the likelihood of her tackling him outside of mine last night is now high. Secondly, this is going to be the most awkward study session ever, but at least it gives me a chance to explain everything to him. Maybe to both of them at the same time. Okay, this day just got a lot harder but that doesn't matter. *Nothing* matters anymore because Ash is back in my life and I don't have to keep trying to move on from him. It's been hell and I finally feel free.

But when Zoe and I walk up to the library entrance and I see Nick leaning against the wall with a takeout coffee cup in his hand, I become massively confused. He actually looks really good, and the memory of our kiss comes into my mind. I bat it away, knowing that I'm with Ash now. Nick just needs to be a friend at most; I can't risk anything and since Ash already knows about our date (which that is not what it was), it's already doomed.

"Hey!" Zoe says, running the last few meters up to him. I lag behind, refusing to run this early in the morning, but Nick looks directly at me the entire time, only pausing to say hi to Zoe.

"You two having a good morning?" he asks politely.

"Amazing!" Zoe says. "We're having a very good morning, aren't we, Harper?"

"Yeah," I say, but I'm not really paying attention to her. The three of us are stood by the door and the silence between Nick and I is heavy. I can tell just by the way his eyes are glowing that he's thinking about last night. He's probably just as confused about it all as I am, but maybe not as much. I'm the one who had their ex show up out of the blue. Nick is just going to be temporarily disappointed that nothing worked out between us but he will recover.

"Come on then, lovebirds!" Zoe says and Nick splutters the sip of coffee he so badly timed. But Zoe doesn't notice; she's already waltzing into the building, leaving me to awkwardly smile at him before following after her.

Zoe finds us a table on the first floor. It's hidden in the corner, divided from the rest of the tables by some bookcases. It's our favourite spot for that reason but I'm surprised it's not been claimed; it might be early by my standards but most students come here before the sun has even risen to bagsy the table they want and start the study grind. Personally, I prefer the few extra hours in bed.

Zoe sits down facing the window, putting her bag on the seat beside her. This is code for *you guys sit next to each other*. And so, with no choice, Nick and I join her at the table, awkwardly apologising whenever we accidentally touch. It's strange to think that less than twenty-four hours ago we had been kissing and now, the idea of even touching each other innocently feels out of bounds. There's so much unsaid between us that I need to get out.

"Right, I'm off to get a coffee," Zoe announces. "Harper, you want your usual?"

"Yes please," I say.

"On it! You two behave, now," she jokes to herself before she waltzes off.

"About last night," I say as soon as Zoe is out of ear shot, turning to face him. He looks at me straight away, as though he expects this. "I'm really sorry. I didn't know that he was coming."

"It's okay," he says and he looks like he genuinely means it. He doesn't even seem uncomfortable about it. "You're not in charge of Ash's actions."

"How do you know his name?" I ask, curious.

"Well, you said it last night before I left," he says and I realise that I'm a bit of an idiot. But I was very distracted last night; Nick was the furthest thing from my mind. "But Zoe confirmed it."

"You guys spoke?" I ask nervously. There's no way that Zoe painted it as a nice picture.

"Yeah," he admits. "She explained the situation. And I know it must have been really hard for you and that's why you had the panic attack at the pub the other night."

I must have suppressed that memory at some point but hearing him bring it up reminds me of how much Nick has already been there for me. It also makes me worried for the first one I'll have around Ash now that we're practically back together again. He never knew how to handle them, or at least not in a helpful way.

"Seeing him last night must have been really stressful," he continues.

"That's one word for it," I cut in. "Sorry."

"It's alright," he says. "It wasn't that long ago when you guys broke up; but I hope there won't be any overlap."

"Overlap?" I question.

"Yeah," he says, taking a deep breath. "I don't know if you and I are necessarily a thing yet, but I think we can both agree that there is something between us, at least?"

Oh no. This is not how this conversation is meant to be going.

"Nick…" I say and he must be able to tell that what I have to say isn't good just by the tone of my voice. He falls back in his chair, combing his fingers through his hair.

"I must have read that really wrong," he says to himself.

"No," I say. "Well, uhm, yes, but -"

What am I saying? Of course there is something between us otherwise I wouldn't have kissed him last night. But what Ash and I have is more than that. It's love. That's what I should be saying right now. That's how I can clear it up. So why aren't those words coming out?

"I know you don't really need to tell me, but could I ask what happened after I left?" he asks. It takes me a moment to think about what he's saying but I must be taking a bit too long because he

106

continues: "I'm not in charge of what you want or what you do in any way, Harper. I just would like to know, if that's okay?"

I take a deep breath and look down at the table. It gives him all the answer he needs.

"Right," he says. "Well, I should probably go."

"What? No, you don't have to leave!" I say, looking him in the eye again.

"You've got some stuff to figure out," he says politely. "You should talk it through with Zoe, okay? I'd still like to be friends, though, if that's good with you?" I nod. "Good. Well, good luck to the both of you; I hope it works out this time."

And he's gone. Nick is gone.

Eleven

When Zoe returns and sees a lack of Nick in the seat beside me, she raises her eyebrows as though she predicted that I'd fuck it up somehow. I hope she's at least surprised that I managed to do it this quickly. *I* am.

"Do I dare ask?" she questions, putting our coffees on the table as she sits down. "Actually, yes, I am going to ask. What happened?"

"He couldn't have just had other things to do?" I ask, even though I know it's a terrible excuse. She tilts her head, willing me to explain. "You can't be mad."

"No promises," she says. "Now, tell me."

I take a deep breath and look down at the table. There's no way I can say this and look her in the eye; just the thought of her reaction is nearly enough motivation to wish I hadn't done anything with Ash in the first place. *Nearly*, but not quite.

"The date - or whatever it was - with Nick was great," I say and before I can cut in, she jumps in with excitement.

"I knew you guys would be a good couple! I'm such a match-maker!"

"I'm not finished…" I say, and her smile disappears. "Nick and I kissed."

"You kissed?! Harper, you saucy devil!"

"And then Ash came…"

"As in, here? On campus? At uni!?" She's practically squatting on her seat in excitement by this point.

"Yeah," I answer. "He knocked on my window and Nick left. Ash asked to come in so I let him and we spoke and…"

"Please don't finish that sentence if you're going to say what I think you're going to say," she warns me. But she doesn't look angry; she looks concerned. I don't even know why I'm scared to tell Zoe. She only ever has my best interests at heart and she'd never leave me alone to deal with anything. She's not like that at all.

"We kissed," I say, letting it float out into the open. I can't help but smile as I think about it. "It wasn't bad, Zoe, I promise. We talked about everything and he said that we might be able to get back together."

"So, he broke up with Abbi?" she asks.

"Well, not yet," I say. "But he loves her too. He doesn't want to hurt her."

"But he can hurt you?"

I want to lash out at Zoe and defend him, but it's exactly how I felt last night when it was all happening. I can't sit here and tell her that she's wrong when part of me is terrified to think of what happens next.

110

What if Ash doesn't break up with her? What if he leaves me again? How on earth am I supposed to trust him again after what he's done?

"No," I say. "No, he can't. But I don't know what else to do! He's Ash. *My* Ash. And he said that he still loves me so I feel like… I don't know… like I need to give us one last try."

"Are you sure he deserves that? Are you sure *you* deserve that?" she asks me. She looks more worried than me and to be fair, I can't blame her. Zoe has only ever seen the bad parts of the relationship; she doesn't know how wonderful it is to be loved by him. "You spent a lot of time crying after the breakup, Harper, but you spent a lot of time crying while you were together too. Do you remember that?"

I think back. I suppose a part of me has suppressed it all but that could just be because at the end of the day, those moments were not important. They don't represent our love as a whole and I don't want them to. No relationship is perfect, so why should mine and Ash's be any different?

"I have to try," I whisper. I don't know if it's the right choice but what I do know is that I can't just let Ash walk away again. I'm not finished loving him yet.

"Okay," Zoe says, holding my hand in hers. "But you have to understand why I'm cautious, yeah? You might have forgiven him, but I can't. I don't want to see you waste away again."

"I won't," I say, even though I don't really know what she means. I've never felt more like myself than when I'm with Ash and that's surely a good thing?

But before I can really think about it, my phone buzzes.

Hey, can u not message for a bit cos Abbi saw it and wasn't rlly happy.

I stare at it, dumbfounded. When Ash and I had been together, I had seen his and Abbi's messages loads; he wasn't desperate to hide them at all. I had to watch them practically flirting all the time while he told me that they were just friends. And I had to stomach that. I just had to accept that this is what I had to put up with if I wanted to be with him. And it was worth it, or at least I *thought* so. But even now, I feel second to her, and all that comes out in reply feels nothing less than petty:

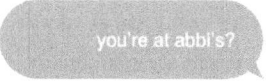

you're at abbi's?

I can't believe he's seeing her; all I can hope is that they've met up so that he can tell her how he feels about me and that they can't be together. But when his reply comes through, that seems unlikely.

i slept at hers.
but srsly, stop
messaging me.

He slept at her house? After he told me he had to get back so his mum didn't worry and he couldn't sleep at mine? *He slept at hers?*

I can't be mad at him because then he really won't want to come back. I don't want him to change his mind already.

"Harper? Are you listening?" Zoe's voice wakes me from my thoughts and I look at her. I barely feel like I'm here, not mentally. It's like someone has just started tearing away at my skin slowly, peeling it to reveal whatever anatomical yuck is underneath it.

"Sorry, what did you say?" I ask.

"Is that Ash texting you?" she says without hesitating. There's no point in lying so I tell her it is. "Is he at least being nice?"

I look back down at the messages. You definitely can't count them as nice by any means, but he's just trying not to hurt Abbi's feelings and I suppose that part is good. At the end of the day, she's going to be just as heartbroken as I was when Ash left me, except maybe not as much because they've not been together as long. They've probably not even said that they love each other yet, even though Ash said it to me within a week. But then again… he did choose *her* over me.

"Yeah, he's being nice," I say, desperate for her not to hate him. Ash and I will have a rubbish relationship if Zoe spends the whole time complaining about him.

"Good, maybe this time he will realise how amazing you are and not fuck it up," she laughs. "But seriously, he needs to break up with her. I don't think you should do anything with him until he does, yeah? You don't want to hurt Abbi. You know how it feels."

"Yeah," I answer. I've already done wrong by her, really. Ash and I have kissed, but we've also been messaging. I can't take those things back, and I don't think I want to, but that line has already been crossed. No wonder Ash thinks I'm an awful person.

"In the meantime," she says, looking around her to check no one is listening. "What are you going to do about Nick? I can't lie, I'm a bit sad you don't wanna go on another date with him. He seems lovely."

"He *is* lovely," I say, sipping my coffee which has by now started to go cold. "He's just not Ash."

"I know that part of you is going to be holding onto the familiarity of Ash," she says, sounding like a therapist. "But that doesn't mean you have to go back to him. You've got a great man right here. He kissed you, Harper!"

I blush, remembering how great last night was before Ash turned up. But it was great after that too.

"He still wants to be friends," I say. "So, he *will* be about, but just not in that way."

"Won't it be awkward?"

"It was one evening," I say. "I'm sure he will be fine."

"Okay…" she says. "I guess we will just have to see how this all pans out. In the meantime, I want all the details and updates about you and Ash. You are going to be blind to his red flags, whereas I'll be ruthless."

"Deal," I say, but beneath the table, I'm crossing my fingers.

***

The rest of the day flies by in a blur of panicking about three things: this essay that is going to be absolutely terrible (I'm calling it), Nick, and Ash. I don't think I've ever failed the Bechdel Test so strongly; two thirds of my current problems are men.

But when I climb into bed and neither of them have messaged me, it makes me wonder. Firstly, Ash not sending a text isn't something I can be fully surprised at; he did warn me. But it does hurt to think about the fact it means he's probably still with Abbi.

But Nick not messaging me? That means he's not as into me as I thought and I don't know why that even bothers me. It's not like I want to *be* with him. I have Ash. I just need to bat it away, remember that it's not important. It's most likely my fear of rejection acting out, rather than any actual feelings for him as a person.

So why do I want him to message so badly?

And why does he have to be the one to reach out? I'm the one who literally rejected him by telling him I was probably getting back with my ex. And I said this the morning after I kissed him!

And so, I curl up under my covers and open up our chat. Our previous messages are there, untainted by Ash coming back, and for a moment, it almost feels like I'm not in this mess. All that's in the air is the possibility of Nick.

> hey!
> did you have a good
> day?

I'm fully prepared not to get an answer, and so when the three little dots appear straight away, I am shocked. In the darkness of room, all tucked up in my blanket, I stare at the screen, waiting with a smile for his reply.

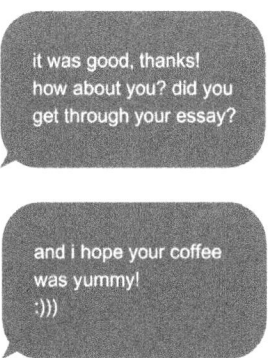

I should feel guilty. The butterflies in my tummy are practically swarming. But not one part of me wants to put the phone down. If Ash can have Abbi, I can have Nick.

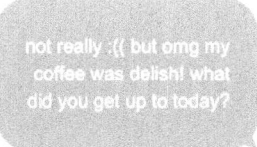

And then… slightly more risky:

> i was thinking about you.

I don't know why I send that last bit. For some reason, I just feel like I need to tell him. Like I want to hear what he thinks about that. Not that it matters. This time, his dots are there a little longer, appearing and disappearing in a small rhythm as though he has to think about what to say.

> did some of my assignment (boring, i know)

> I was thinking about you too

Nick and I keep talking for a few more hours and I'm practically squirming in excitement with every new one he sends through. And after a while, Ash drifts from my thoughts, and when I fall asleep mid-text, he's not the boy I'm thinking about.

Twelve

I wake up in the morning with my phone stuck to the side of my cheek. I prise it off, knowing I'm going to have the strangest red mark on my face for a while. But for a moment, it seems completely worth it as I remember how long Nick and I spoke for last night. The only problem? I think I just cheated on Ash.

I power it on to check my notifications. There's nothing from Nick, but it must be because I fell asleep with our chat open. There are definitely new messages:

it's one of those books where you have to read it twice, i think.

you good?

awh.
did you fall asleep on me, harper?

have a lovely sleep xxx

He's so lovely that I can't tell if I should find this massively cringey. But I don't... I feel guilty.

Ash has only just told me that we could be getting back together, that everything can go back to normal. So why am I trying to sabotage that before it even happens? There's no way he will want to be with me if Nick and I do anything together. Even last night was pushing the line and that was all done in innocence. But I have to end it now. I have to do what's best for Ash and me.

hey, i think last night was a mistake. we can only be friends. sorry :(

At this point, I don't want him to reply straight away. It will just make it harder for me; it'll be obvious that he likes me a lot more than I like him. Not that I like him at all. I like Ash.

But he disappoints me, answering within a minute of my message going through.

> i know you have a lot going on so please don't worry about me!

> you just look after yourself, okay?
> xx

It's strange how supportive he is. I'm rejecting him right now... where's the anger? The complaints? The silent treatment so I can realise that what I did was wrong?

There's none of that. It's just Nick being Nick.

But it just reminds me how there isn't a message from Ash. It's not like I deserve one after how I practically cheated on him last night, but it would have been amazing to wake up to a morning message from him. I know he's up already because he always does the morning shift at his work; he has to be up and out of that door for 6:30am most days.

Maybe today is his day off... but he hasn't been at work for a few days so that seems unlikely. But there must be some reason and I have to be okay with that. He won't want me back if I'm the same anxious mess I always was with him; he'd be back in Abbi's bed before we even started trying to make things right. So I have to be strong. I have to be strong for Ash.

I drop a quick reply to Nick, thanking him and letting him know I'll see him in class. I don't want to dwell on him, the kiss we had, or the fact that we texted for hours. I want to move on quickly to bigger and better things, and, now that I know Ash wants me, I can start focusing on my uni deadlines properly.

But before I can do that, I get myself ready for the day. I put on a fresh pair of jeans and a low-cut white top, wanting to be able to look in the mirror today. I pair it with a matching jewellery set and comb my hair back, applying only a small amount of makeup. For the first time in forever, I don't feel like I need more.

When I walk out of my room to go for breakfast, I bump into Zoe and she does a bit of a double-take.

"You're…?"

"Presentable?" I laugh back.

"You just look happier," she says. "Oh no. What did you do?"

"Why do you think I did something? I could just have slept well; you don't know," I say as she follows me into the kitchen. I know that she won't leave it until she knows all the details. It makes me a little nervous because I almost know that she won't fully

122

approve, especially when she finds out that I've practically led Nick on like an absolute idiot.

"Is it Ash?" she asks. And I don't say anything, but I *do* smile and she knows I'm guilty. "Were you guys talking last night?"

"Well," I say. "Sit down and make us some breakfast and I'll fill you in!"

"So cheeky!" she says, but she loves to cook. She'd happily make every meal for the entire flat if we'd let her and if our mealtimes lined up. And so, when she starts getting out all the ingredients for pancakes, I become instantly excited. I haven't had them in so long; they were always something I linked to Ash because he used to make them for me all the time. "I figured these are a safe food now he's back?"

"Definitely!" I say. "I have missed them so much! I hope you can cook quickly."

"I can't exactly ask the batter to work faster," she laughs back. "Now, come on and tell me what's got you so rosy this morning."

And so I tell her about last night. I tell her about how Nick and I spoke for literally hours and if I hadn't accidentally fallen asleep mid-conversation, we probably would have kept it going until the sun came up. And I tell her about this morning; about how lovely Nick is and how horrible I am. But I leave out about how I'm scared of Ash and what he will do if he ever finds out. Zoe can't know anything about that stuff; she will just talk me out of my guilt by

123

putting Ash down. And that's not fair on him when I'm the one who's causing him hurt and he doesn't even know it.

"Well, that was a lot," she says with a deep breath. She looks like she's unsure of how to react but I know she's simply brewing up a reply. She dishes up another pancake, sliding it onto the table in front of me. She's so motherly; I don't actually want to know what uni would be like if we hadn't been placed in the same flat. It's strange to think I've only known her for a few months and she's already my closest friend. "So, you're telling me that you have spoken to Nick nearly all night?"

"Yep."

"And then Ash was at Abbi's..?

"Yes," I say, more reluctantly this time.

"And somehow you're happy about the second part?" she looks at me, a mixture of pity and confusion. And that hits me.

"It's Ash, Zoe," I say, like that answers everything. But as soon as the words fall out of my mouth, I realise that they don't. They don't even get close. "It's Ash." I try again.

"You've got a lot to figure out," she begins, starting the next pancake. "A lot has happened this week and I don't envy you at all. If Ash really wants you though, he will break it off with Abbi. But don't you forget that he cheated on you with her while you were together. He can't just erase that."

124

"I know," I say. "It's okay." I don't know if I believe that but if Ash and I have any chance of being together, I have to at least try. I can't keep holding it over him.

"As long as you're fine with it," she says. "Don't hate me because I *have* to say it, but are you sure it's Ash that's made you so happy?"

Normally, I'd throw back a defensive comment without hesitation. But I actually think about it, just to make sure her point doesn't have any meaning behind it. Last night was great; Nick and I can clearly just talk about anything and everything and it comes naturally. But I have that with Ash too and as soon as we move past this whole Abbi thing, we can go back to being like that again. All of this mess will be worth trudging through. I just have to be patient; Ash is my happiness and it always comes with a price, right?

"Yep; he'll sort it all," I say, more so to convince myself than Zoe. But she's just looking out for me, and, after all, I did promise to keep her up to date whether my fingers were crossed or not.

"Well, while you're in a good mood, no matter what the cause of it is," she continues. "You want to go out tonight? The Literature Society is going to a bar to do karaoke if you feel up to it? Megan and Kelsey are coming, and I think that means that Michael will be too."

"And with Michael comes Nick," I add.

"Most likely," she adds. "But there will be loads of people there so I'm sure it won't be awkward! Maybe you could invite Ash?"

"But he knows about Nick... not about *everything*, but he knows that we had a date," I say, worried. "Not that it was a date."

"Keep telling yourself that," she says. "But seriously, you can't stop your life because of Ash being a jealous dick, when he literally boned another girl while you were together. And you can't even complain at me for that; I'm just talking honestly. But you should be able to invite your maybe boyfriend to things like this."

"You're right," I say. "I'll ask him after breakfast. He might have work, though." I add this last bit to help give him an excuse, just in case he can't come.

"He works the morning shift so nice try."

Zoe listens to me too well. I need to be more careful about what I tell her; she clearly doesn't forget anything. Which, I suppose, I should feel grateful for. But honestly, it just scares me.

"I'm just saying," I say. "It's last minute."

"Yeah," she adds. "But it's just an invite. Now, eat up your pancakes and then we are going to feed the ducks."

"Feed the ducks?" I ask, confused. It's so random. It's literally a Thursday. Part of me thinks it's a euphemism for something but when she picks up this week's loaf of bread, I realise she's really not kidding.

"No point in it going to waste!"

126

"You're so odd, Zoe," I say, shaking my head. "I hope you are aware."

And so we go to feed the ducks, literally. And it's nice to be outside, even if it's a little cold and my fingers turn red after only a short while. But it helps me feel lighter, almost like I can forget about everything that's going on.

But throwing bread onto the ground doesn't undo anything that's happened recently. It doesn't change the fact that I'm yet to invite Ash because I'm scared of how he'll answer. And it doesn't change the fact that part of me is disappointed that Nick and I can only be friends. But that's why I don't deserve Ash at all; not one bit.

Thirteen

Zoe is insisting that we go all out for the karaoke meet-up. She's been rifling through our wardrobes with Megan, both of them acting like the 'Simon Cowell's of the fashion world. *No to this, no to that. Definitely not that.* I'm starting to think that I don't actually have anything worthy when Megan pulls out the tiniest dress I think I've ever seen.

I'd actually forgotten about it. I'd hung it up just to keep it nice, but I never looked at it. Why would I want to be reminded of *that* night? But looking at it now, held out across Megan's body like she's shopping for her own outfit, I see it all and wince.

***

"I've got a surprise for you," Ash says. I've only just got to his and this is literally his opening line. No 'hello', or 'how are you'.

No, Ash is so much better than that.

"Oh, yeah?" I say, smiling as he brings me in for a hug. He smells so good that I could happily spend the rest of the afternoon just in his arms, tucked up all safely.

"Yep! Come with me and close your eyes!" He guides me to his bedroom door, making me even more nervous every time I stub my toe on a corner or half-walk into a wall. "Okay, I'm just going to close the door behind us, so keep your eyes closed!"

"I will!" I say. By this point, I am so curious to know what's he's done that's got him this excited to show me. It's like being a child on Christmas day, charging in and ripping open the presents.

"Hold out your hands," he says and I do so, laying my palms flat out in front of me. He places something there almost immediately… something light… a fabric of some kind. But I don't dare move my hands to feel the shape. "Okay, you can look now."

I open my eyes and they fall directly to my hands.

"Ash!" I say, looking at him in shock. "You didn't!"

"It's for tonight," he says. "For the party." He looks so proud of himself, so happy with the one that he chose. I let it fall between my fingers, getting a better look at it. It'll be short on me, that's for sure, because it's one of those club dresses. The tight ones that hug you. "I thought you could do with a little black dress."

"Wow," I say, unsure what to say. I can't believe he bought me a dress?! I can't believe he bought me anything, but I'm holding the evidence in my hands. "This is so nice of you, Ash."

130

"Do you like it?" he asks. I hesitate in getting my words out, but he doesn't give me chance to succeed. "I saw it and I just pictured you in it. There was no way I couldn't buy it for you after that. I literally got a boner in the shop."

"Why were you in the girl's section?" I ask, looking him dead in the eye. He hates shopping; he always complains when I ask to go but he went optionally?

"Just with mum," he says but he shuffles his feet and ignores all eye contact. "So, you'll wear it tonight?"

"Of course I will."

***

No part of me wants to wear this dress. Even though Ash is absolutely lovely for coming back and being here, nothing can erase *that* night. But I can't say that to the girls... maybe to Zoe, but even she doesn't know about it. So I nod.

"Yeah, that's good," I say, gulping. Megan practically throws it to me.

"Fab! Pair it with your black heels and you've got one hell of an outfit there," Megan suggests but she's already started heading towards my door, dragging Kelsey to her room for her turn. Zoe raises her eyebrows at me, rolling her eyes in a smile.

"You'll look great in that," she says to me. "You should send Ash a picture; maybe it will kick his ass into gear. Has he replied yet?"

I never even sent the text. Why would Ash want to come to a random karaoke for a society at a uni he doesn't even go to? With people he doesn't know or like? It just feels like a disaster waiting to happen, so I've avoided asking at all. But sending him a photo isn't a bad idea…

"Not yet," I say.

"Hopefully he will see it soon," she says. "Otherwise he won't be able to get here in time. Anyways, I'm going to get ready. You good?"

"Yep," I say. I'm not sure if I am but I just need to hold myself together for a few hours and then I can crawl back to my bedroom and see if Ash can call. I want to talk to him so badly, but what I really want to know is if he has broken up with Abbi yet. It's all that I can think about and it's scaring me. What if he doesn't? What if she already knows and isn't letting him leave her? There's so much that can go wrong but I don't deserve for this to be easy.

So I get myself ready to go out, slipping into the dress just like I had done all those months ago. It feels weird, but that might just be because I haven't done my makeup and hair yet; that usually makes all the difference.

But even after I've finished with those, I look in the mirror and feel the exact same.

I feel exposed.

I feel naked.

***

The girls and I arrive at the bar, all of us just as dressed up as the others. Megan is in the smallest red dress I've actually ever seen in my life, and she's done this 'fox-eyeliner' for the both of us so that we could be 'twinsies'.

Kelsey has gone for a floral dress; she's definitely a comfort kind of girl and I can relate to her there.

Zoe, on the other hand, has gone for a full on pant-suit look with those vests that show cleavage; she looks so classy next to us three, almost like she was due to present on a show after the event.

And then there's me. Ash's dress hugging my body. The navy blue sparkling under the lights of the bar, making me feel like there's no possibility of being invisible tonight. It's even worse because of the fact my hair is curled into this 70s style blowout, and with the extravagant make-up look Megan's done for me, it all feels like so much.

My point is proved quickly when we walk up to Michael and Nick, and neither of them can get a word out.

Michael is staring directly as Kelsey, looking more smitten than the last time that I saw them together.

"You look amazing," he says, holding his hand out. She takes it and they begin their own conversation on the sidelines of the group.

133

Zoe nudges my back, and it's all too obvious what she wants me to do.

"Hi," I say to Nick, barely able to hold his eye contact.

"Hey," he says, his voice heavy.

"Right, well," Megan cuts in. "Zoe, come and help me add all our names to the karaoke queue!"

The two of them waltz through the crowd, leaving me alone with Nick.

"You look beautiful," he says. "Different, but beautiful."

"Thank you," I say, looking at my shoes.

"Is Ash coming tonight?" he asks. It sounds as though it was hard for him to get it out but I can't blame him for asking.

"No, just us guys," I reply, sending this information out into the air, making the fact I didn't even invite him sit heavy. Maybe I should have? Maybe I need to show him that I want him to be involved in my life? But I know that I can't deal with the rejection that would come if he is still with her. That would hurt more.

"Cool," he says. He looks relieved. Which, to be honest, I would be too. Ash can be scary, and even though they've never really met, Nick knows that this boy literally came all this way and knocked on my window on the off chance of seeing me. I'm sure it's clear to him how much Ash wants me, how much he'd do to keep me.

134

"Are you looking forward to karaoke?" I ask. The conversation feels quiet, feels dry. It's weird; I'm comparing it to how we spoke the other night. But then again, it was just the two of us then, hidden behind our screens while it was dark outside. Here, we're just two people in the middle of a massive uni event.

"Yeah, I guess," he says. "I love music, to be fair. I play guitar, you know?"

"You do?" I say, genuinely shocked. "Me too?"

"No way!" he laughs and we're back to normal. "Do you write music too?"

"Sometimes," I say. "But not a lot recently."

"Maybe you'll find some inspiration soon," he adds, and the pragmatics hang between us. "I'm in a band too."

"Seriously?" I say. "I didn't know you were so cool."

"Ouch!" he says.

I'm about to come back with an equally witty comment when someone pushes into me, spilling their drink all over my heels and knocking me into Nick. He catches me easily, and looks to the guilty man beside us:

"Watch out, man," he says.

"Sorry!" is the reply but he's gone before anything can kick off.

"It's okay; it's just an accident…" I say, though the sticky alcohol on my feet doesn't help.

"Shall we go and get you cleared up?" Nick says and I look at him desperately, on the verge of laughing at the situation.

"Please," I say and he guides me through the crowd to the bathrooms.

"I'll stand guard and wait for you here," he says as we reach them. "You go on in and get sorted."

"Thanks, Nick," I say. I lock myself in the bathroom and before I can even think about cleaning my feet, I throw my face in my hands and smile at the thought of him standing outside. I have no idea what is happening but maybe tonight won't be as bad as I thought it would be.

***

When I emerge, I'm half-surprised to see Nick there, still waiting for me just like he'd promised.

"You all good?" he asks and I nod, a massive smile across my face. I can't even hide it, even though I should. I shouldn't be smiling at another man at all. But I'm happy… and Ash isn't here. He's probably with her, if I'm really honest with myself.

Which maybe I need to start being.

"Let's go find the others," he says. "I'm sure we'll be up for karaoke soon. I wonder what songs she put us all down for?"

"I think I have an idea…" I know exactly what Megan will pick, especially because Zoe was there too for the song choices. They both know I love to

136

sing, and they've all heard me blasting this one particularly loudly multiple times. It came on during a fresher's party back in term one and I was the loudest singing along. Strange; I'm usually so quiet but music always calms me. I'm like a different person, which is why part of me is glad Ash isn't here.

I can focus on me for a change.

Fourteen

When we find the others, they are stood by the front, watching a small group of girls singing along to "Sweet Caroline" on the little stage. They have their arms linked around each other, beaming into their microphones and laughing in between the lines. I always hope that this is what my friends and I look like when we're together... happy. But I feel like I'm maybe letting us down there, walking around with my miserable face. Zoe is always reminding me that I'm allowed to feel that way; I've been through a lot and I'm just trying to survive it.

Still, I wish I could be happier for everyone else's sake.

"What a performance!" the DJ says and everyone cheers, shouting around me. "Next up, we have Megan!"

Megan runs up onto the stage, taking the microphone and whispering something into the DJ's ear. Who knows what she says, but he shakes his head smiling.

"Hey everyone!" she screams and we all scream back. "I'm going to sing an absolute banger for you all!"

And just as she finishes speaking, the song starts to play. We all recognise it immediately…

"She just loves the stage, doesn't she?" Nick says to me. He's stood beside me, close enough to touch if we wanted to. But I don't want. I don't want. I don't - *well*.

"We always joke that she should have done a performing arts degree of some kind," I say to him, slightly louder to be heard over the music. "But for some reason, she's a book nerd like us."

"She doesn't look it," he says.

"And what does a book nerd look like, then?" I ask, teasing him. He looks at me, and for a second, his eyes drop down to my lips. All of a sudden, I'm reliving the other night when we kissed and I think he might be too.

"Like you," is all he says. "But not tonight. No, tonight you're something else, Harper."

I don't know how to react but luckily I don't need to.

"Does no one dance anymore!?" Megan shouts down the microphone, jokingly furious at the lack of audience participation. "Come on! Don't leave a girl hanging!"

And so… we dance.

Together.

"Oh my gosh!" Zoe says, sliding on over to us. "Look at you two!"

"Shush you," I say, elbowing her. "And dance with me!"

140

Zoe and I fall into Megan's song, moving together and letting loose. I haven't felt this free in so long; my brain is fully distanced from Ash and Nick and uni and everything. The only thing that matters in this moment is having fun with my friends, laughing and enjoying our time at uni like you're supposed to do. It's normal.

I'm normal.

And then Megan's song ends and my name is called. I rush up onto the stage, too clouded by the atmosphere to fully grasp what's happening.

"Hi guys!" I say, surprised at my confidence. I haven't even had a sip of alcohol... I just feel so alive. "I actually don't know what I'm singing yet because my gorgeous friend Megan put me down for a song, but hopefully I won't bugger it up!" Everyone cheers up at me, and I look down at my little group in the front row. They all look so happy. So *excited*. And they're mine. These are my friends... my people. I'm okay. No matter what happens with Ash, I'm not alone.

And then the music starts playing and I give a sigh of relief when I realise my guess is correct. I'm so glad she didn't choose tonight to pick a completely random song and watch me embarrass myself. But I don't think Megan would do that; she may be a bit extra, but she's never mean.

As I start to sing the first few lines of Taylor Swift's *Never Getting Back Together*, I fall into the lyrics completely. I used to play it all the time when I was twelve, meaning every line as though I'd actually had a relationship and knew exactly how it all felt. But performing it now, I can give it a different kind of energy because I've loved now; I've gone through a breakup. And so every word that comes out of my mouth and through those speakers is real.

When I get to the second verse, I look down at my group again. Only this time, I'm looking for one specific face.

Nick.

He's looking directly at me, his eyes twinkling under the lights, his smile illuminating his face. He looks so cute down there. So cute I could almost kiss him.

And then I do something I maybe shouldn't do, but this is what happens when you get caught up in the moment. I climb right off the stage, holding the microphone limply by my side as I kiss him. I don't care what people think. I don't care that everyone's probably looking at us right now, thinking how insane I am.

All that I care about is kissing Nick, feeling his lips on mine.

And when our faces pull apart slowly and I see his face, I know it was all worth it.

"What was that?" he asks. "Not that I'm complaining." He adds this on the end, rolling his eyes playfully.

"I couldn't help myself," I answer. "I just had to."

And I pull myself from his arms, heading back onto the stage for the final chorus. By this point, the crowd is so alive and loud; I must be a better performer than I thought. But the only person in the crowd that matters is Nick... and the fact that I probably just changed everything for either better or worse. Who knows? But it felt right and it still feels right.

As the song finishes, I hand back the microphone, beaming as I climb back down onto the floor. Everyone's crowding around me, asking me a million questions about what on earth has just happened, but all I can focus on is Nick. He's stood on the outside of the group, looking at me all adoringly. I hold his eye contact, smiling softly at him.

"What the actual fuck, Harper?"

I whip my head to the side and see the worst person I could possibly see right now.

Ash.

He's seen it all. He's seen me kissing Nick. He's seen me looking at Nick like he's my boyfriend, like I love him. And I had completely forgotten about Ash and our agreement, or whatever it was. I still don't have a clue what's going on.

"Are you gonna explain, then?" Ash continues. "Or do I need to do something about it?"

I look at Nick. Concerned, my breathing becomes heavy. But he doesn't look phased... he's not exactly buff to any degree, but neither is Ash. A fight between them could go either way and I don't want to find out. Mainly because I don't want either of them hurt.

What have I done? I've ruined what I have with Ash over a moment? Over a night of texting and one small kiss. Over another boy. Gosh, why is this all *so* confusing?

"Harper?" Ash says. I can practically see the flames flaring from his nostrils and the steam around his head; I've really gone and messed it up this time. He's never going to forgive me. He's never going to want me.

"Can we talk?" is what comes out of my mouth. And once it's out there, I don't even know if it's the right thing to say. But what else can I do? Walk away and ignore him? Throw everything we had together away over someone I just met?

But Nick's right there, being all lovely and gentlemanly and calm. And I'm a few feet away, being a broken piece of junk; he could so much better than me. He doesn't even look mad. *Why isn't he mad?*

"I think we better," Ash says, storming from the building.

"I'm sorry, guys," I say to the group, but mostly to Nick. "I need to sort this out but I'll be back soon."

They all give me pitiful looks and Megan practically dotes on me with a hug before I can join Ash outside.

"So?" he says, leaning against the brick wall with a scowl on his face. He can barely look me in the eye

144

and it hurts so much. It *really* hurts. Seeing him holding himself like that against the wall reminds me of the other night at the pub, when Nick had taken me outside to get some air. It feels like a lifetime ago now, just one memory that I've lived and is now in the past.

"I didn't mean to," I begin. "It just happened in the moment; we were all having a good time."

"So cheating on me is a good time, is it?" he spits back.

"What?"

"I just told you that we could be getting back together and you're out here tonguing some random guy behind my back!"

"I know," I say. "I *know*."

"That's messed up, Harper," he adds.

"I know," is still all I can say. I burst into tears, shocked at how emotional it's making me. Once again, I look like an absolute idiot on the side of the street.

"Do you still want to even be with me?" he asks.

"Yes!" I jump in. No matter how confusing this all is, I know that I *want* him. This is *my* Ash! My first boyfriend, my first love. I've been reckless; I need to slow down and remember how much he means to me.

"Right," he says. "Then we need to get a few things straight. Firstly, I don't want you hanging out with that guy."

"Nick?" I ask. I can't be surprised; his request is perfectly normal after what he's just seen. But the idea of not talking to Nick ever again makes my stomach fall. He's right, though; he's the guy I cheated on Ash with. He *has* to go. "Okay," I submit, but it comes out in a quiver.

"You also have to answer your fucking messages," comes the next part of the deal.

"Yeah, that's fair enough," I admit. "I'll keep a closer eye on my phone."

"And if you're going out, then I'm coming too," he says, looking back at the bar. "Otherwise you're not going; you can't be trusted."

This one feels weirder, more invasive. But he's got a point; I did kiss someone else here. But I also spent a whole night messaging Nick that Ash doesn't even know about yet and surely that's just as bad? I shouldn't even tell him; he'd go crazy and he'd be incredibly mad.

"Anything else?" I ask. I realise it comes out harsher than I meant it to when he throws me a deathly glare.

"I'll let you know," he says. "In the meantime, we are going back to yours."

"What?" I say, suddenly standing up straight. "I'm with my friends, Ash."

"Yeah, and you kissed one of them!" he shouts. "Do you know how that makes me feel?"

I didn't even think about Ash in the moment. That would be weird, though… thinking of another

146

boy during a kiss. But it's exactly how I feel about Abbi and I know how awful that feels.

And I've done the same damn thing to him.

"I'm sorry, Ash," I say, hanging my head. "I shouldn't have done that. I'm *really* sorry."

He huffs but holds out his arms: "Come here, you."

I hesitate but end up tucked into his chest all the same. I can feel his heartbeat. Slow. Steady.

The complete opposite of mine.

Fifteen

Ash held my hand tightly the whole way back to my dorm room. He was even reluctant to let go when I had to unlock the door to the flat.

And now we're sat on the bed again and I'm wondering what's going to happen. I'm glad that he's here but I'm so scared of what he might do. He's angry with me at the moment, even if he stopped telling me ten minutes into the journey back, and I know how he can be when he's mad. I shouldn't have done anything to provoke him, but how was I supposed to know that he would be there? Come to think of it, I still don't know why he *was* there. This isn't even *his* town. Abbi doesn't live here. It makes no sense.

"Ash," I say, taking a deep breath. "Why were you at the bar?"

As soon as I ask the question, it hangs in the air over us. It's suffocating but I have to know.

"You're still sharing your location," he says simply. When we were together, we always shared our locations with each other. Me for safety and him because he could. I guess I just forgot in the midst of everything going on to turn it off.

"So, you're stalking my every move?" I ask.

"Oh shut up, Harper," he says. "Can you blame me? The two times I've come here, I've caught you with the same guy. Once, he was here in your room and you were doing God knows what. And then tonight you were kissing him in a bar."

Well, that silences me.

"I want to trust you," he adds, more gently this time. "But I just can't do that straight away, you know? You have to give me time."

"You *can* trust me," I say, desperately. "I just can't be sure you actually want this, Ash. Have you even broken up with Abbi, yet?"

"Not yet," he says, brushing my hair behind my ear and kissing my forehead. "But don't worry about that. I love you both but you're the one I want, Harper."

And, like no time has passed, like the last few days didn't happen, we're kissing again. It starts soft, romantic, calm. But once he gets comfortable, his lips press against mine harder; his way of proving me to how much he loves me.

But this doesn't feel right. I can't help but think about Nick, back at the bar with the girls and Michael, how we kissed in front of everyone, how I felt so damn happy.

And now I'm here, hidden away behind walls, kissing another girl's boyfriend because he *used* to be mine. And it makes me feel sick; I don't know why but it does. But I can't pull away; what would that tell

Ash? That everything I just said was a complete lie? No, my only option is to lean into this kiss just as much as him and show him that he can trust me. That I'm all his.

***

When I wake up in the morning, I realise that he's still here. Our clothes aren't; I don't know where they ended up. But he is.

He didn't leave.

"Good morning, beautiful," he whispers into my hair. I must have woken him up when I moved.

"Sorry," I say. "You go back to sleep."

"I've been awake for ages," he says, pulling me in more tightly and wrapping his hand over my head. He strokes my hair gently and I sink into the safety. This is my favourite version of Ash; the one who is soft with me. "I wanted to let you rest so I've just been enjoying holding you."

"You're cute." I blush. "What time is it, though? Because I have an early class today. I did have an alarm already set in case I forgot after going out; I wonder why it didn't go off?" I lift my body up, leaning over Ash to reach my phone.

"I turned it off," he says. "I didn't want anything interrupting our time together."

"Ash, this is my degree?" I question him.

"Aren't I more important?" he bites back. "Aren't we more important than some silly little piece of paper?"

"It's not a competition," I say, wonder-struck at how quickly he has changed. Only a few minutes ago he was holding me close, being all sweet and lovely, and now *this*? I don't understand it at all. But I reach over him and grab my phone. The light blares on, revealing the time. "I have fifteen minutes to get there!"

I practically fall over him, rushing to climb into whatever clothes I pull from my wardrobe first.

"Harper, come back to bed," he says, looking at me with doe eyes.

"Ash, seriously!" I say, not even bothering to look at him; I can't waste any time. "I just told you that this is important to me. You shouldn't have turned my alarm off without my permission but that's already done. But what you *can* change is how you're being now. You have to go!" I pick up his t-shirt from the floor and throw it in his direction. I don't have time to regret it.

He lunges forward, grabbing me by my wrists, holding them tightly up in front of me. His eyes furrow down at me and I cower beneath him.

"You don't tell me what to do, Harper," he spits.

"I'm sorry!" I burst. "Please let go; you're hurting me!"

"What did I literally *just* say?"

152

I look into his eyes. Those same eyes that usually look at me with so much love. So much care.

There's nothing like that in them now; he's furious. Mad. Angry. Terrifying.

"Not to tell you what to do," I echo back at him. "But you can't *hurt* me!"

"You cheated on me, Harper," he says. "It was a test and you failed."

"A test?" I question, so surprised that I stop struggling, my eyes darting back and forth between his left and right, trying to figure out what he means.

"When I came over and saw Nick at yours, I was fuming," he explains. "You were moving on."

"You moved on before we even broke up!" I say, and he tightens his grip.

"That's different," is his excuse. "I can't just leave Abbi without knowing if I can trust you, can I?"

"But I have never done anything to make you question how I feel about you," I say. I'm so confused. So, so confused.

"You kissed another man last night, Harper," he says. "It's barely been any time since I said that we might be able to get back together and you thought you'd ruin everything? Do you even like him? Or are you just using him to make me jealous? Cos if it's that, I get it, okay? But you don't need to make me jealous because it's you that I want."

"So, you'll leave Abbi? We can be together for real?"

153

"No, not yet" comes his answer. Blunt and direct. "I can't trust you, but Abbi is a great girlfriend. I can't risk losing *that* until I know that *this*, whatever it is, is worth it."

I don't understand what he's saying but I know that it hurts. I also know that it's entirely my fault. This is all happening because of how I've been with Nick; of course Ash doesn't trust me. I wouldn't trust me, either, because I did the exact same thing he did and that broke me.

"I get it," I say slowly. "I *really* do get it. You're right; I shouldn't have kissed him after we spoke. But please let go of me." I look at him, pleading with my eyes. If I show how much he's hurting my wrists, he might just do it.

"Only if you promise you won't speak to him," he says. "I already asked once and I don't want to have to ask again."

"I won't," I say. I try not to think about what he's asking me to do; it will only make it harder and it's best to suppress everything that could have been and nearly was… and think instead about how to gain Ash's trust. He drops my hands, which I suppose is a good start.

But it's not enough.

"Ash, what *are* we?"

It's one of the hardest questions to say but I know that we can't keep going on as we are doing. The lines are so blurry and it's just going to lead to more

154

fights like this if we don't know what the boundaries are.

"What do you mean?" he asks.

"I mean, what *are* we?" I ask again, not sure how he expects me to make it any clearer.

"I'm with Abbi," he says, as though it's unchangeable. As though he's not shirtless in my room after a night of doing whatever he wanted. "I'll break up with her soon, when the time is right."

"So, we aren't together?" I ask.

"Technically not," he adds. "But we don't need a label. People only use those when they're insecure."

That sounds like the end to it. No matter how much I push, he's not going to change his mind on this. I'm going to have to play the long con, convincing him as quickly as I can that he can trust me and that we are meant to be together.

"I should go," he says, finally putting his shirt back on. "Remember not to text me, yeah? I'll let you know when I'm free to talk."

"Okay," I say, crossing my arms over my chest.

"We're in this together, okay?" he comes back over, as though he had just remembered me again, kissing me on the forehead. "You look so beautiful."

"Thanks," I say, though I don't feel it and I know he's most likely lying; my hair will be such a mess and my makeup from last night will be smushed around my face. But I can't argue with him; I can't make it worse.

155

"I'll see you soon, yeah?" he says. "And no talking to Nick."

"I won't," I say, not knowing if I fully mean it yet. I watch as he leaves, closing the door behind himself. Listening out for each of his footsteps along the corridor, I hear him close the front door. I stay there for a while.

Frozen.

Thinking.

Scared.

PART TWO

Sixteen

As the weeks go by, Ash and I spend less and less time with each other. There's always something that he has to do, or someplace he has to be. But I get it, because he has a busy life and I am a whole train ride away; I'm not exactly close by. But I do wish he'd come over more, or at least let me come to his. He's just always so worried about Abbi bumping into us or finding out.

They did break up, though, this morning. Just when I thought it wasn't going to happen, too...

***

pick up your damn phone

I read his message, looking at all the other ones he has sent before. The essay deadline is literally tomorrow and Zoe and I are sat in the library now, trying to get through these last few hours and scrape at least a pass.

"Do you want me to keep your phone in my bag?" Zoe offers.

"It's okay," I say. "I'll just remind him about tomorrow. Say I really need to focus."

I start typing out my reply, hoping that he will understand, but as soon it comes through, three little dots appear. It won't waste too much time to just wait and see what he says, how he reacts, but he's not even talking about my essay at all.

i just broke up with abbi.

I stare at those six words, questioning if they are even there. In my doubt, I point the phone at Zoe and she reads it; I'm surprised she can as my hand is shaking so much.

"Finally," she rolls her eyes. "I wonder what she said."

"It doesn't matter," she says. "She originally stole him from me, remember?"

"Yeah," she says. "You better not forget that either. But I guess now you have to ask the big question."

She's right; she's so right. Ever since Ash slept at mine, I've been scared to bring it up. Scared to rock the boat a little too much now that our paths were lining up again. I've been playing it safe. Hoping for *the best. But now is the best time to bring it up and I can't deny that.*

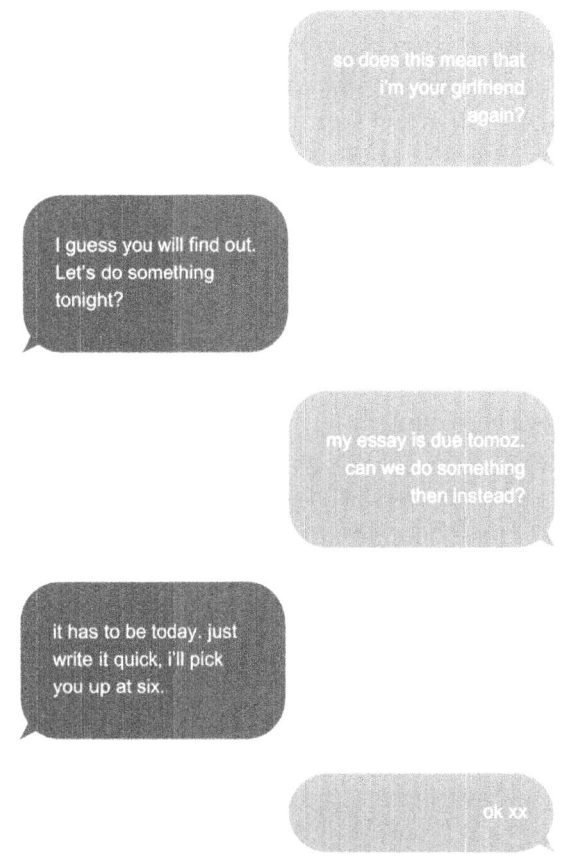

so does this mean that
i'm your girlfriend
again?

I guess you will find out.
Let's do something
tonight?

my essay is due tomoz.
can we do something
then instead?

it has to be today. just
write it quick, i'll pick
you up at six.

ok xx

"I think he's going to ask me out tonight," I say as a small smile escapes onto my face. "Right, he's getting me in like three hours so we need to focus."

"I've been focused this entire time but you do you," Zoe laughs. *"You want a coffee top-up?"*

"Please!" I say, sinking back. I'm grateful for how calm she's being; her hatred for Ash hasn't disappeared over the last few weeks, but she has kept it to herself. And it's made a massive difference in keeping me calm throughout all of this. And now, it feels like it was all worth it.

***

It's hard to believe that it only happened this afternoon and that I'm now sat on my bed in jeans and a nice top waiting for him to knock on my window. It's already past six... by about twenty minutes. I know he will be here though; stuff like this excites him. There will be some logical reason why he's not quite here yet, and I'll laugh about it later.

Finally, I hear him knocking and I rush over to my window, opening it and beaming.

"You ready, beautiful?" he says.

"Yes! I'll come out now!" I go to close the window again but he holds it still.

"I'm trying to be romantic here," he says but I don't understand. "Climb through; I'll catch you if you fall."

"I am not climbing out of a window, Ash," I laugh. But he looks deadly serious, as though me not doing this ruins everything. "You really want me to?"

164

"I wouldn't have asked if I didn't," he says, this time more bluntly. But he clears his throat and continues: "Come on, you're good." He holds out his arms and I stare at them… he's just trying to have a bit of fun. I don't know why I'm being so weird about it.

"Okay, let me grab my jacket and my phone," I say. I collect them and pass them through to him; something tells me that it will be easier to squeeze between the panes without a bulky coat on. I'm quickly proved right as I slither over the ledge, but luckily Ash is too busy guiding my body down onto the ground to notice how awkwardly I manage it.

"Well, I like having you this close," he whispers from behind me.

"Ash! We are literally outside like six blocks of accommodations right now," I tell him, pulling myself from his body. "You can be a pain later on."

He seems content enough with that answer so I'm safe now; the happy version of him will be around for a little bit longer.

"So, where are we going?" I say.

"Follow me," he says. And that's when I notice the suitcase by his feet. It's not huge by any means, but there isn't a valid reason why he should have one right now. He could literally just bring a bag if he needed anything.

"Ash, why do you have that?" I ask, pointing at it.

"If I tell you, it's going to give away the surprise," he says. "Don't worry; it's nothing bad."

I follow him through campus like a little puppy at his heels, asking him every few minutes if he could possibly give me a clue. But it's always a 'no' and a knowing grin, and eventually I give up. But all the patience leaves my body when we reach the train station.

"Are we going to yours?" I ask, knowing it's only an hour away. But that wouldn't explain why he has a suitcase.

"Nope," he laughs, tightening his grip on my hand. By this point, I'm becoming more worried; I don't know what he has planned but it's looking more and more extravagant. I should be happy. I should be grateful. I've wanted him to step up for so long and he's finally doing just that, but the timing is all wrong. For one, he only just broke things off with Abbi this morning; there are things that we should be talking about. Serious things. And the other thing is that my essay is due tomorrow at noon. I wrote as much as I could before going back to mine to get ready, but I'm still a few hundred words away from the minimum word count. I figured I could just go for another round in the morning and give it a last minute push. But that can't happen if Ash's plan goes into tomorrow.

"Where are we going, Ash?" I ask. I suddenly realise the situation for what it is. It's dark outside, I'm by a train station with someone who's technically not even my boyfriend anymore. I can't trust him. I can't trust *me*. He has a suitcase?!? This is actually really scary. "You *have* to tell me. I'm not getting on any trains before you do."

"You're gonna ruin it, Harper," he says, pulling us to a stop. "I've planned something really nice and it was actually really expensive. So can you please just shut up and be grateful? I could have just done nothing."

"I'm sorry," I say. "I just - my essay."

"Didn't you finish that thing?" he asks harshly.

"Nearly," I admit. "I just need another two hours or so to get it done. I was going to do it tomorrow morning."

"Well, this is why you shouldn't have left it till last minute," he says. "That's on you."

I don't have the heart to tell him that it was his fault it took me so long to start. After he left, I was so broken that doing basic things felt impossible, let alone writing detailed essays that are hopefully worthy of at least a pass. And then when he came back into my life, everything became so confusing, so heavy, that the words didn't come easily. It's been such a long process of just trying to make a little bit of progress; he has no idea how much I've had to push myself to even get this far. But I can't say that. He won't like it. And he will just say that it's my fault we had to break up, which I suppose it is. If I had just been good enough in the first place, he never would have needed Abbi and I don't need the reminder.

167

"Okay," I say. "Let's go." The words come out quietly; part of me hopes he will hear the reluctance in my voice; he will then give in and tell me what his plans are. I don't like the idea of just hopping on a train, going somewhere random, no one knowing where I will be apart from the two of us. It's stupid, I know. I've known him for so long but something just feels wrong... I don't know what has changed in the last month, but something must have. For all I know, I'm probably just scared to lose him again; it's the only thing that makes sense in all of this mess.

"Finally," he says, continuing to head into the station. The sound of his suitcase wheeling across the bumpy pavement grates in my ears, and I feel like I'm suddenly aware of all the noises going on around me. It's isolating but overwhelming... a whole world is ticking by; all the billions of people are doing their own thing, and I'm here with Ash: something I never thought would happen. Knowing this reminds me that I need to suck up any anxieties I have and just try to be the best girlfriend I can be for him. That must be what tonight is leading to; him asking me out. And now that he's left Abbi, he's really shown how much it's me that he wants and I can't waste that.

"Hey Ash," I say.

"What now?" he spits back, but neither of us stop walking. Whatever train he's booked must be leaving soon.

"Thank you for this," I say. "It really is sweet of you."

168

This brings him to a halt. "No problem." He says it like he's thinking, like little clogs are turning in his head. But he ignores them and continues to march. I follow after him, trying to hide the utter terror on my face as we enter the station.

It's busy here, especially since rush hour has ended. It only makes it easier to sneak between the crowds of people; hopefully no one will notice how scared I'm looking and think that Ash is kidnapping me or something. But it also makes it harder to figure out which train we're getting on. There are multiple platforms, I think eight, and announcements are blurring above us. Neon letters flash on the screens, shifting and changing as though the trains are leaving much faster than humanly possible.

"Give me your phone. You've got the train app downloaded, right?" he asks.

"Yeah," I say, passing him it in confusion. He's probably just going to transfer the ticket to make it easier to pass through the barriers. But when he hands it back, I couldn't be more wrong.

"Just bought yours so we're all good," he says.

He didn't even buy my ticket.

"Uhm, thanks," I say.

"Don't look at it, though," he adds quickly. "It says the location on. I wanna keep it a secret as long as possible."

"Okay," I say. I watch him go through the barrier first and I try to glance at my screen quickly to get a glimpse of the name. But he turns back around so fast that I don't even have a chance. All I can do now is scan it and join him on the other side.

"Come on you," he says. He holds out his palm and I go to place my hand in it when he pulls back. "No, your *phone*."

"What, why?" I ask.

"So you don't peek at the ticket," he explains. I hand it over; this is a valid excuse, after all. "This is our platform." He guides me into the train and offers me the window seat. He knows I hate sitting in them; they make me feel stuck, like I can't get out if I need to. But his words from earlier flash in my mind: I can't be ungrateful. So I take a seat, watching in worry as he puts the little suitcase in the carriers above my head. He slides in next to me, holding onto the top of my thigh. "I'm so excited, babe."

"Me too," I feign.

But all I can think about is how stupid I'm being. Why on earth do I feel so uneasy?

Seventeen

Once we are all settled in our seats, Ash insists that I put his wireless earphones in so that I don't hear any announcements saying the name of the place he's taking me to. It's sweet, really, how determined he is to keep it a surprise. It must be someplace really good too, since this train is incredibly busy.

It becomes a little boring though after a while. Ash's music taste is completely different to mine and every song sounds exactly like the one that comes before it. I can't even try and strike up a conversation with him because he's sat on his phone, holding it at just a big enough angle that I can't see the screen. At least *he's* entertained.

And all this waiting has me over-thinking about my essay. Whenever Ash lets me have my phone back, I'm going to have to text Zoe to submit what I have so far, just in case. Or maybe I'll have her email a copy so I can write when I'm out. I really want to get a good grade on this assignment. Other than the fact I've spent over a month on it, I also just want something to be excited about. I want to feel as though I've achieved something. But then it seems absolutely awful to be mad at Ash for the fact I might not be able to finish it... he's *right*. I need to stop leaving things until last minute. It only comes to bite you later on.

Finally, Ash starts standing up, sliding the suitcase onto the floor before holding his hand out to me.

"Can I take the earphones out now?" I ask. He chuckles a bit, nodding. As I'm taking them out he says to me:

"Yes, but you don't need to shout."

"I didn't?!" I say in horror. The music must have been so loud in my ears; that's so embarrassing.

"Right, if you don't see the signs telling you where we are, you'll definitely be able to tell now anyway," he says. I stand up behind him as we head to the door.

"I can't wait to find out!" I reply, because a part of me is actually really excited, uni deadline or not.

And as soon as I step out from the train, I know exactly where Ash has taken me. And I start to cry.

Because he really does love me.

"Hey!" he says, noticing my tears and pulling me into a hug. "Are you okay? You weren't supposed to cry..." He adds this last bit as though he's confused.

"They are happy tears, I promise," I say. "You know how much I've always wanted to come to London."

"Of course," he says, messing up my hair. "I thought it would be a nice way to celebrate."

"Celebrate?" I ask.

172

"That you're my girlfriend again," he says. "Come on you! Let's go to the barriers."

I follow after him without thinking too much about my movement; I just trust that I'll be okay as I grip onto his hand. But all I can think about is how my expectations have been a little bit dashed. I thought he was bringing me somewhere romantic so that he could ask me out again in the sweetest way possible. But apparently we're just naturally together again. It's my own fault, really; I shouldn't have assumed.

I've never been to London before but it's something I've wanted to do for years. I thought that it would feel as though I already know everything, like I'll recognise places and streets. But all I can think is that it's just so… big.

We haven't even left the station yet and it's like I'm in the middle of a crowd of thousands, each person on their own little mission that's a part of their daily schedule. Ash leads me past them all, guiding me through the gaps that seem only momentary. And suddenly our faces meet the fresh air.

"That was a bit chaotic," I say. It was kind of overwhelming, but in a good way, as though I was living for the first time. Everything is always so slow in our home town as it's only small, and uni is just your stereotypical campus. But here? It's so loud, so busy, so real.

"That's London for you," he says. "Right, we can check in whenever but I'm thinking we should go get some dinner while we're out?"

173

"Check in?"

"To the hotel," he says, as though it's obvious. It wasn't, but at least I know for definite that I won't be back in time tomorrow to work on my assignment. I really do need to message Zoe about that. And, to be honest, I need to tell her where I am in case anything happens. But now doesn't seem the right time to ask for my phone back; we only just got here. I'd look ungrateful and he doesn't deserve that after planning such a thoughtful trip.

"Okay," I say. "What do you fancy?"

"I could go for a burger," he says. I kind of hoped he'd flip the question back on me, since he's taken me here so I can finally have my London experience. But in his defence, I literally asked him; all he did was answer.

"Burgers sound good," I agree. "Where can we get those?"

"There are probably about five burger places down this one street," he says. "But it will be more fun to hop on the underground to Soho. You in?"

In all my research about London, I know that Soho is the food hub of the city. I also know that it is a lyric in a Maisie Peters song. And that's where my knowledge ends.

"Let's go!" I say.

"Right, you gonna be able to keep up?" he asks and I furrow my eyebrows. "It's fast-paced down there. Don't get lost."

Now would be a good time to ask for my phone. You know, in case I actually *do* get lost and can't find him. But he's already dragging me towards the station and there's no point in trying. He's excited… *I'm* excited. What can go wrong?

As we reach the underground, I notice how it's pretty much the same as the train station, only smaller. It's basically just an entrance: a row of escalators taking people up and down constantly. And now I'm a part of it all. I'm stood on the right-hand side, as I've always known you're supposed to do so that people in a rush can get past you. Someone actually does that too! I almost lose my balance but I'm so sandwiched in between Ash and this random dude behind me that my body just rocks against them. It feels a bit wrong to be touching a stranger, even if it is completely innocent and an accident, but I'm sure he doesn't care in the least; this is all probably normal for him. But Ash would, so I'm glad he can't see it.

We finally get to the bottom, which is great timing because I'm beginning to feel all dizzy, and there's a labyrinth of passages and signs pointing the way to the different lines. I trust that Ash knows where he's going; he certainly looks it. And he stands us on a platform.

"This is so cool!" I say, noticing the tracks and the darkness that looms in the tunnel.

"Just wait until the train comes," he says into my hair. I can literally hear his smile and it makes me blush. I'm so happy and relieved that everything is working out again! I don't know why I've been so worried and why I've been constantly thinking about Nick. Ash is my person and this trip is making that clearer with every minute.

Then, awaking me from my thoughts, the train blasts past us. It doesn't seem possible that it can slow down in time, but it does, and a cloud of people squeeze through the doors.

"Don't let go of my hand," Ash says, pulling us to the front of the mess of people so we can get a place in the carriage. It seems unfair to cut past everyone who was here before us, but when I look out the window and realise how many people weren't able to get on, I see why he did it.

"Is it always this busy?" I ask.

"It would've been worse about an hour ago with rush hour," he says. A few more words come out of his mouth but I can't hear a thing now that the train has started to chug forward.

"It's so loud!" I scream. He just smiles and shakes his head, as though I'm the cutest thing he's ever seen. Damn, I missed that look.

But Nick did kind of do it sometimes…

"Not this stop!" Ash shouts as it slows down again. He brings me closer to him, holding me tightly. "Don't want you going with the swarm."

"Good idea," I say, finally able to hear him. We're so close now and I don't care that we are on a tiny little carriage with about fifty other people. I'm

176

never gonna see them again. And so I kiss him. I kiss him like it's the last time, like we'll never see each other again, like the last month didn't happen at all. Because Ash is my boyfriend again, I'm his girlfriend, and everything is how it should be.

But there's something dry in the kiss as I pull away. He's not even looking at me anymore; his eyes are on his phone which he has pulled out of his pocket with the arm that had only just been around me.

I'm too upset about Ash's behaviour to care when someone wolf whistles at us. Of course I can hear *that* over the raring noise of the tracks and not Ash properly.

He puts it away as quickly as he had got it out in the first place and even though I want to know more than anything what he keeps checking, now is not the time to have that conversation. Neither of us would be able to hear anything and the fact I keep getting thrown about as the carriage jolts won't help.

"This is ours," he says, this time with less energy. He doesn't even hold onto my hand this time to make sure I get off safely. Instead, he expects me to sift through the people and then follow him down the platform; his body gets further and further away as new people come between us.

"Ash!" I shout but he doesn't hear me. He must think I'm still behind him.

I begin to push past people, throwing apologies into the air; I can't lose him. I don't know where we're going, I don't know how to get out of the station and I don't have my phone! This is looking like a terrible idea now; we shouldn't have come to London. I shouldn't have gone back to Ash. He can't even make sure I'm safe when we're out and about together. That doesn't sound like love…

And then there is Nick, who literally recognised a panic attack and took me outside, waiting with me in the night air until I was ready to go back in. God, I've been so horrible to him! I never even properly explained to him why I had to stop speaking to him. He didn't deserve that.

I reach the top of the stairs where Ash had disappeared up, but he's nowhere to be seen. All I can really do is follow the signs for the exit and hope he hasn't gone to another platform. There's probably a worker there who can help me, who could let me borrow their phone.

But when I reach the top, I don't see him anywhere. And, unfortunately for me, this place seems a lot busier than Euston station. He could be standing literally steps away from me and I won't even be able to pick him out from the crowd. I just need to stay calm and trust in him a little bit longer. Then I can figure out what's going on in my life for it to make me feel this confused, scared and just downright rubbish.

For now, I have to accept the fact that I'm lost and alone in London.

178

Eighteen

Just as I'm about to ask to borrow someone's phone to ring for help, a hand grabs me from behind.

"There you are!" Ash says, looking as though this isn't a big deal; it's simply a funny little accident to him. "I lost you down there."

"You just kept walking," I say slowly, more in realisation than anything else. It comes out almost broken, and all I can feel is disbelief at his actions. Has Zoe been right this whole time about him being terrible? About him being bad for me?

"I thought you were behind me!" he says, his face looking like he's surprised I'm trying to pin it on him. But of course I am; he *left* me!

"You could have checked. And why do you keep looking at your phone?" I ask. I don't even regret asking; I'm so annoyed. He thinks he can get away with everything just because I never call him out on things. But this was dangerous; this is worse than all the other stuff that I don't understand. "And you've got mine! I couldn't even text you. Speaking of, I want it back now. We're here; your excuse isn't valid anymore." I hold my hand out in front of me, trying not to back up and undo all of my words in case they make him angry. It's so hard to stand up to him but he should care enough about me not to leave me stranded in the biggest city in England without a phone.

"Calm the fuck down, Harper," he says.

"No, I want my phone," I tell him. I try to keep a strong face, to show him that I'm serious this time. But all I want to do is break down and cry because he's scaring me.

There.

I admit it.

He's scaring me.

"I'll give it to you later," he says. "We're going to get food now. You don't need it." He grabs onto my hand so tight that I can't wriggle it away. But to anyone walking by, we just look like a normal young couple holding hands with each other; no one will see this as a problem... as something that I don't want.

But watching him walk away from me in the underground and realising he wasn't there when I got out, reminds me of all the times he used to disappear before. Before Abbi. Before the breakup. Before everything.

***

He still hasn't replied to my good morning message and I can't stay up much later; it's already past midnight and I've got a class early in the

180

morning. But it's making me so anxious, not knowing what he's doing, who he's with. And the last text he sent was so dry that I could die of dehydration.

I'm lying here in bed, in the darkness, with our chat lighting up my face. If I stare at it for long enough, I feel like I can will him into replying.

But it never comes.

This always happens. Everything is completely fine. We laugh. We smile. We love each other like people do in relationships. And then, all of a sudden, nothing. He's been active on everything; he even sent out his snap streaks around lunch time. So that means that he's actually choosing to ignore me and I don't know what I've done wrong.

I retrace all my steps; I think about everything I said to him yesterday… there wasn't anything problematic. But I must have done something, otherwise he wouldn't want to avoid me. I just wish that he would tell me, because if I know, I can do something about it. I can show him how sorry I am and how much I love him.

Almost all of me wants to just ring him, but I know he'll decline the call. He won't even bother to let it go to voicemail before he shuts me down. He never does.

And so I lay here, alone in the dark. Waiting.

***

Somehow, I manage through another day. I sent a second message after I woke up, just in case he's simply forgotten to reply. But he opens it straight away and ignores that one too. I half hoped to at least see the little dots at the bottom of the screen, but I don't even get that much.

By the time the evening rolls around, I feel sick. I haven't even told the girls yet because I don't want them to see him as a bad boyfriend, but they're all going out for bowling now. They invited me, but I said I'm not feeling well. That will cover up how pale I look from worry. And they all buy into it. They all believe my lie.

But now I'm alone again, waiting for a message that I don't even know will come. I check his Instagram, and our pictures are still there; I'm still in his bio with a little heart emoji; to the world, we look perfect. Like nothing is wrong. But on the inside, it's so messy.

I run to the bathroom and hunch my body over the toilet bowl just in time. I don't even know how I've managed to be sick because I haven't eaten a single thing in two days, but the smell tells me that it's real, somehow. I curl myself up in a ball, just crying at how unfair this all is. About how I'm the most terrible girlfriend and I don't even know why. About how Ash could have anyone he wants, and he's chosen me, but I'm letting him down.

"Harper?" Zoe says from the bathroom door.

I don't know how long I've been here; my brain is running at two hundred miles an hour trying to make sense of it all. But she runs to be by my side, flushing the toilet when she notices the sick; I probably should have done that myself. I'm so gross. So undeniably gross and awful and terrible and what on earth is Ash doing with me?

"What's happened? Are you still not feeling well?" she asks, concern flooding her face in the way I wish Ash's would.

"Ash," is all I get out before my tears choke me.

"Hey, it's okay. It's okay." Despite the fact I've got vomit across my lips, she pulls me into her chest, stroking my back in circles and combing my hair with her fingers. "It will be fine. I promise."

***

Looking at him now, I realise that this is the same person. This is the exact same Ash who had me feeling like that.

And I didn't make myself cry.

"Ash, I want to go home," I say.

"What? No, we only just got here!" he complains, still dragging me through the crowds. "Just stay the night. It will be good."

"Ash, please!" I beg him. "I want to go!"

At this point, he pulls me to the side, standing us by a shop window selling swimsuits. He hovers close by, quietening his voice.

183

"Why do you want to go home?" he asks. He's talking like he's trying to control his breathing, as though he could lash out if I provoke him anymore. But part of me feels safer doing it here, out in the open, where he can't do much to hurt me.

"Because you're not listening to me, Ash," I tell him. "You won't give me my phone back. You physically dragged my here. Look at my wrist!" I hold it up to him, seeing for the first time his finger marks that are burned into my skin. I freeze, realising how bad it really is. "You hurt me."

"Look," he says. "I'm sorry, okay? But look at it from my perspective: I planned this great surprise to celebrate us getting back together and you're being ungrateful. That hurts *me*."

"That's completely different to leaving a mark," I say. I can't believe he's trying to wiggle his way out of this; has he always done this and I've just stupidly trusted his words? I'm such an idiot.

"Maybe I shouldn't have done that," he says. "But please can I just take you to this restaurant so we can have a nice night? I'll make it up to you, yeah?"

I don't know what he means by that, but I can take a guess.

"I don't want you to do it like that," I whisper. I hate it when he treats sex like a game, like it's something I owe him just because he's my boyfriend... something he can do instead of apologising.

184

I always use to think that but I don't think I do anymore. Because the idea of it is more terrifying than the thought of being alone in London. "Please just take me home." This time it comes out a little squeaky as I begin to cry.

"Don't fucking embarrass me, Harper," he says. All the softness he has tried to muster throughout the conversation is completely gone now as he bares his teeth. How can nobody around us see what's happening? How has nobody stepped in? My last bit of confidence dies as I cower beneath him, my body shaking in fear at how angry I've made him. "We are going to go to this restaurant. Then, we're going to go to the hotel that I've paid for, and you *will* enjoy it. You get that? Because I lost Abbi to be with you and you're starting to make me think I've made the wrong choice."

I nod because I don't even want to try and reply properly.

"Good. Now, stop crying," he orders and I wipe away my tears. He holds out his hand and I stare down at it; for the first time, I realise how much I give up constantly to be able to be with this boy. I give up my *safety*. "Hold it."

I hesitate but I know that I don't have a choice; I'm too deep in now.

And I let him walk me to the stupid restaurant. I let him order for me even though I've always said that salads are a waste of money because they don't fill me up. I let him eat his burger in front of me

185

as he complains about how I'm vegetarian and it makes everything so much harder. I let him talk and talk and talk.

But most importantly, I let him think I'm sorry.

"That was so good," he says, wiping his mouth with the napkin as he finishes the last bite of his burger. "Was yours okay?"

"Yes, thanks," I say. My plate is completely empty; there was no way I was leaving a single morsel for him to pick out and complain about.

"Check please," he says as a waitress walks by. She looks young, maybe our age: a uni student with a part-time job to get by. And he looks at her. On *our* date, right in front of me, he looks at *her* as though he's thinking dirty thoughts.

"Of course," she says with a smile. She disappears for a minute before returning, placing it down on the table. "Who will be paying?"

"That would be me," he says, sitting up in his seat and leaning into her smile. He pulls out a card from beneath the table and I notice the red of it between his fingers: it's my card. He's using *my* card. "The man always pays, you know?"

"How chivalrous," the waitress says as Ash scans it. I can't believe he just did that… "Thank you; that's gone through. Have a great evening." She's not looking at me at all. And then, after she walks away:

"That's for earlier," he says, excusing the fact he just used my money without consent, using the card I keep in the phone case that he's practically stolen

186

from me. "Now, let's go to the hotel. It's only down the street."

I don't know how it got this bad. Maybe he's been like this all along? But none of that matters now; I have to get my phone back and I *have* to get help.

It hurts to realise it but I don't want Ash in my life anymore. I don't want any of this.

Nineteen

Ash signs us in at the reception and I'm just grateful that it's the first thing he hasn't charged me for. First, the train ticket: that was different, almost acceptable. But then the meal at the restaurant? That was just pure anger and him trying to put me in my place. That's going to be a lot harder to move past. Part of me is waiting for him to ask me to do a bank transfer to pay for my portion of the hotel room but for the few minutes we've been here, he hasn't mentioned it.

He doesn't even bring it up when we scan into our room, four floors up. He lets me in first, holding the door open for me to pass through, and then slots the little card into place for the lights to come on. I hear the click of the lock before I even have chance to venture further, not that I need to worry. If, for whatever reason, I have to get out, I can just as easily turn it to the side and I'll be free. But it's just the sound of it, echoing in my mind, symbolising how he's between me and escape.

"You excited?" he asks me, as though we didn't just argue in the street. I nod my head, not wanting to disappoint him.

"Yeah," I say. "Did you bring anything for me?" I add, looking down at the suitcase. His smile grows large, a cunning twinkle in his eye, and I wish that I hadn't asked.

"We will get to that later," he says. "In the meantime, we should shower. I hate feeling yucky from travelling."

"Sure," I say, kind of agreeing with the statement. But it's more than the trains I want to wash from my body right now. "Do you want to go first or me?"

"We always used to shower together," he says, confused as to why I didn't just assume that.

"We haven't been 'together' for a while, Ash," I say. I cradle my arms together, hoping that if I just explain how I'm feeling, he will understand. "It's going to take me a while to get used to being close again."

"You didn't seem to have a problem with that whenever I came to yours," he argues back. But he was different then. Or, maybe not different, but it wasn't as bad. Things have changed and the idea of sleeping with him now feels like absolute hell. "Look, we don't have to have sex now. I just want to shower and be close with you, yeah?"

I know he's trying to make it sound better but he's dancing around the point. We both know what he wants and we both know that he will probably get it… because I can't say no to him. When did it become like this? When did it all change?

190

And suddenly, in a guilty sort of way, I think about Nick.

I don't want him like that, like I once wanted Ash. But I think about him, as a person; how he never made me feel pressured to do anything, or how he just wanted to make sure I was okay. Those things don't necessarily mean anything, though, because Ash used to be like that at the beginning. When we first fell in love, he was there for me when I was struggling; even if he didn't like having to deal with them, he always helped me through my panic attacks. So, no; Nick probably would have turned out the same.

And what's the common denominator in both of those situations? Me.

"Harper?" Ash's voice rings through me. My name sounds like nails to a chalkboard as his question rubs against my brain; I try not to squint from how uncomfortable I am.

"Yeah, we can do that," I say. Because what damn choice do I have? I've learned tonight that you can't just go against Ash; if he wants things to pan out a certain way, he'll get what he wants. And I've been the idiot who's fawned after him all of this time because I'm scared to be without him, scared to be alone. But I'm starting to think that maybe they are the better options.

So I follow him into the bathroom and I watch him turn the shower on. The water sprays out quickly and just seeing it makes me feel nauseous. There's no way out of this now, though. I have to see it through until I can figure something out and he can't keep me in London forever. He can't afford to, for one. And then, as soon as I'm back at uni, I'll tell Zoe everything and she will know what to do. I have to keep reminding myself of that, reminding myself that I'm not alone. I have Zoe and Megan and Kelsey and maybe even Nick and Michael too, if I didn't mess that up too much.

"I've missed you so much, Harper," Ash says, cupping the sides of my face in his hands. He's so close to me that once upon a time, maybe not even too long ago, I would have kissed him here. I'd be all giggly about how cute it was and I'd just melt into his touch. But that touch feels like acid now, tingling against my skin. "I was stupid to let you go." He kisses my forehead firmly, as though he's saying goodbye. But this is only just the beginning.

I won't describe the next ten minutes; I don't even want to think about it, let alone relive it completely. Every moment that I've had to spend with him tonight has been more difficult than the one before it and it's starting to feel like the day will never end.

But it has to eventually. That's what I tell myself as he wraps me up in a fresh towel, taking his time as he weaves it around my body. I can feel his fingers through the fabric and I try not to pull myself away; I can't make my discomfort too obvious. I need to keep him calm because he's better then. Nicer.

192

"You ready to see what I packed?" he asks.

"Let's go," I say, trying to feign my most believable smile. He guides me back into the bedroom and unzips the suitcase on the bed. It takes only a few seconds for that zip to go around but I wish it had taken much longer.

"I bought them especially for you," he says proudly, taking some pyjamas out and handing them to me. "I know how much you love the colour purple and I think it looks really beautiful on you."

I'm shocked. Full on shocked.

I expected something dirty, like lingerie, or at least something small and tight-fitting. But these are just normal. They will surprisingly cover a lot of my skin and they have a really delicate floral pattern.

"Ash," I say, the words failing me at first. "These are actually really nice."

"What do you mean *actually*? I have great taste in women's clothes," he jokes and I shake my head.

"I am so sorry for how I've been tonight," I tell him. Holding the pyjamas in my hands makes me realise that I probably pushed it too far; I got ahead of myself, assuming the worst in him. We haven't been together properly for a while and so it's bound to be a little rocky as we get back into a rhythm... as we learn how to be in each other's spaces again. "I've been so ungrateful and I think I'm just self-sabotaging because I'm scared of losing you again."

"It's okay," he says, looking down at his feet. It's like all his confidence has disappeared. "I'm sorry

193

too. I just got worked up because it felt like you were ruining something I was really excited to do for you."

"I get that," I say, putting the pyjamas back in the suitcase so I can hold his hands. "I really am happy you brought me to London. It's the most romantic thing that anyone has ever done for me."

"Well, that's a bit meaningless considering I'm the only boyfriend you've ever had," he says, tilting his head with a smile. "But I'll take it all the same. So, I was thinking that we both get changed and curled up. Then, we can channel surf until we find something decent to watch? It might take a while, though, because it is a hotel TV after all."

"Sounds good to me," I say. "Did you at least pack me a toothbrush?"

"Bought us a new pack completely," he says. "I think it's gross bringing your one from home around with you."

"Agreed," I laugh. I rifle through the suitcase until I find the toothbrushes and toothpaste and then I take them off to the bathroom. Ash decides to join me at the sink and, for a moment, we look like a normal couple. We are just a pair of teenagers in love, spending time with each other, being happy. And, although he scared me a little earlier, I know that he isn't a bad person. At least, not always. Sometimes, he's like he is now: perfect and sweet and funny. That's the Ash that I love and that's the one I've been fighting for this whole time. It's a relief to believe that we got through it, that we found our

194

way back to each other. But it doesn't matter how it happened; what's important is that it has.

Once we finish, he playfully races me to the bed and we both land with a massive thump. He's on top of me now, our faces close.

"I really want to kiss you now," he whispers.

"Okay," I say softly back. And so, I lean into him as our lips touch. He's soft at first, all romantic and slow. But it doesn't take him long to show much he loves me; his tongue pushes against my lips, prising them apart so he can explore.

This is the bit I never like.

I haven't told him that before, so I can't expect him to know, but there's just something weird to me about including wet tongues. Like, it doesn't make sense. But this kiss is different. If I don't enjoy it, then what does that say about how much I want Ash to be my boyfriend? I'll tell you what it means. It means that there's something wrong with me. There's this amazing boy who wants me and is proving that, and for some reason I want to throw up.

But I let him kiss me for as long as he wants, *how* he wants. I owe him that much after how I've treated him today, even if I still can't fully process everything that's happened.

He finally pulls away, his lips smiling against mine.

"I love you, Harper," he says, as though it's a conclusion to the kiss.

"I love you too, Ash," I tell him back. Because I do. I *do* love him and I was being silly earlier. So damn silly. "I love you so much."

"Let's get ready for bed, yeah?" he asks. He finally releases my body by climbing back from the bed and I realise now just how much he was squishing me that entire time.

"Okay," I say. I take the pyjamas back out of the suitcase and hold them in my hands awkwardly. Do I change here, or should I go to the bathroom? I don't think I feel comfortable doing it in front of him, but if I do it elsewhere he might ask why and I don't have an answer.

But once I start to change, I realise he isn't even watching me. He gets into his own pyjamas and then sits in bed on his phone. I climb in beside him, trying to peak subtly.

"You ready?" he says, noticing me. He puts the phone face down on his lap over the duvet.

"Yeah," I say. "Could I have my phone?"

"Why do you need it? We're supposed to be spending time together," he answers.

"I know," I reply. "But I really need to make sure my essay is sent in on time. I'm going to ask Zoe to submit it from my laptop, but if we can, I'd love to go back really early tomorrow so I can write a bit more."

"So, you want to end our trip early so you can do something you should have done ages ago?" he asks me. He doesn't even say it in a mean way; it's more so just a comment on the situation.

196

"I know; I should have done it ages ago! But I didn't and so I really need to do this," I say. "Please, I'll just message her that and then I'll put it away and we can snuggle in?" I phrase it as a question, hoping he can see how desperate I am.

"Alright, be quick," he says. He passes it to me and watches as I unlock it. I can still feel his gaze on it when I pull up Zoe and mine's direct messages and I'm just grateful that neither of us had said anything bad about him the last time we texted. But I drop her a message and hope that she can read between the lines. Or, at least, realise that this is a stupid decision and become worried anyway. It was always so annoying when she did that before because I wanted her to love Ash as much as I do, but I need that fire in her now so I can get back in time for my deadline.

All I can do for now is wait for her reply and hope that it comes through soon.

Twenty

Ash finds a random film quickly enough, something about zombies running around chasing people. Basic boy stuff really. I don't really mind what we watch, to be perfectly honest. I'm quite happy just cuddling up with him, waiting for Zoe's reply about submitting my essay.

We are about twenty minutes into the film when my phone buzzes and I look at Ash knowingly. He passes me it without hesitation and I'm glad that it didn't have to turn into anything big again; I really don't have the energy and I only just managed to calm down after it all.

> idc what you and Ash are up to! Tell him this is important...

I tell her this information in a way that Ash can't find annoying. I'm not begging her for help, or complaining about being here in London. I'm just reacting to the situation: replying to her message. And it's a good job I do too, because he's reading every single word on the screen right now, making sure I'm not doing anything silly.

But then his phone buzzes and he's distracted for a moment. I could try and send Zoe an honest message, saying that I don't think Ash will actually let me go home in time, but then he might see it.

"Right, we should head to sleep," he says, putting his phone back on the side-table. I put mine down on the one on my side, hoping that if I put it away myself he won't see a need to. Luckily, it works. "Good night, beautiful." He kisses my forehead and crawls further under the covers. "Turn the light off, will you?"

I do as he says; the switch is only next to the bed so it's not exactly a hard thing to do. And then we're in darkness. Me and him. Ash and I. I look over and see the silhouette of his back moving up and down slowly from his breathing; he's probably already asleep. I swear it's a superpower he has; being able to fall asleep instantly. It's kind of annoying sometimes, though, because I always want to chat for a bit before bed but he's gone within a second. It was something that I got used to, and I guess I'll have to get used to it all over again. But for now, I curl up behind him, being the big spoon because I know he likes it.

But no matter how long I lay here, waiting for sleep to come, nothing happens. Ash starts snoring after a while, so I know that he's out like a light. But for some reason, I can't do the same. My mind is both overwhelmed and quiet at the same time. No thought can stay long enough for me to really process its existence but I know they are there, floating around, begging me to make sense of everything. But how am I supposed to have all of the answers right now? I can't. I *really* can't. I don't know how Ash had it in him to leave me, or why he came back. I don't know why he cheated on me and then decided it actually was me that he wanted. I don't know how he can go from hurting me to being all lovely.

And I don't know why I think this is okay. But I don't think it is bad enough to be something to worry about; other girls have it so much worse. They're beaten and raped and shouted at... Ash just loves me in the only way he knows how and that means that sometimes he isn't perfect. But it's not bad enough for me to be complaining about. It's not bad enough for me to run away.

201

And then, my phone screen lights up on the bedside. Thank god I didn't have my sound on, because it would have woken Ash up. I reach for it slowly and dim the brightness so it won't disturb him, and I want to vomit.

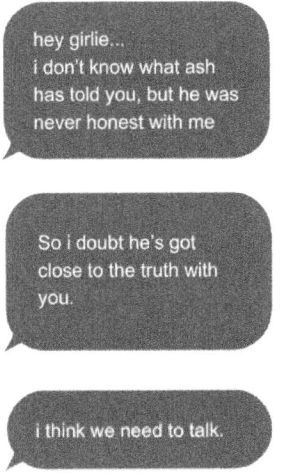

> hey girlie...
> i don't know what ash has told you, but he was never honest with me

> So i doubt he's got close to the truth with you.

> i think we need to talk.

How did she even get my number?

The more times I read it, the more confused I become. I look back at Ash beside me, peacefully sleeping as though he could do no wrong, and I look down at the words on the screen that tell me the opposite.

What do I do? I can't exactly ring her up and have a full on chat about my boyfriend right next to him. And I should *trust* him.

But I don't think I do.

202

No matter how much I want to, I don't.

After what happened this evening, I feel like everything I thought about him has been completely dashed. The boy laying beside me is someone else...someone mean... someone who can hurt me.

And maybe that's why I reply to Abbi: because I want some damn answers.

> now isn't a good time.

I don't know why I don't expect it, but I'm shocked when she answers straight away. She barely gives me enough time to process that I've replied... that I'm going behind Ash's back.

> tomorrow afternoon? i'll train to you. we can meet for coffee.

This is the moment where I decide mine and Ash's future. No, *seriously*, there is so much pressure and it feels like there's a right and a wrong choice. If I don't go, I'll never know what happened between them and whether or not I can trust him, but if I do meet with her? Ash will be so upset. *I'll* be upset, because it will mean that our relationship isn't perfect.

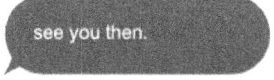

That gives us plenty of time to be back in time; there's no way he will make me stay longer than that, surely?

see you then.

I don't even know if I should be concerned that she knows what uni I go to, but in true twenty-first century fashion, she probably stalked me once she and Ash got together, just to make sure that I wasn't going to get in the way. It's a bit weird, actually, now that I think about it. Ash cheated on me with her, but he came back to me; she must feel just as awful as I felt back when it happened... Or she is a complete witch and in that case, tomorrow could go a very different way to how I first imagined it.

But I can't do anything tonight, so I put the phone back down on the bedside table and fall asleep, quietly crying to myself.

***

"Good morning, you," Ash says, cuddling me from behind. His breath is warm against my neck and I brush my shoulder against him, wanting to carry on snuggling the pillow so I can sleep. "I thought you wanted to go back early?" he says with a teasing tone.

"What time is it?" I muffle through the covers, keeping my eyes tightly shut.

"Eight something," he says. "If you get up now, we have time to pick up some breakfast on the way to the train station."

"I thought you didn't want to go back early?" I ask him, curious enough to turn over and face him. It's been so long since we laid this close to each other peacefully, still enough for me to see the blue in his eyes. It's moments like these that make me question everything because they prove how lovely he can be. For a second, it even makes me forget about Abbi's messages last night... but the guilt of not telling him about it creeps in.

"Yeah, but I thought about it and your essay is more important," he says. He finally gets it; he understands... Almost every part of me wants to tell him to forget it, that I just want to lay here with him, being close and in love. But I have to make the mature decision and go back for the sake of my uni grade. I don't want to fail because of a boy, or because of who I become when I'm with one. "We can spend the weekend together, yeah? I'll come to yours."

"Sounds good," I say, embracing his kiss. It's small and delicate; my favourite kind.

"Right, let's get ready, little miss sleepy!" he laughs, rolling out of bed. I wake up too, though a little more slowly, and we get ready to leave. Today feels so different, almost as though the light outside has made everything literally brighter. But it's weird, comparing all of his movements so far to how he acted yesterday... is it as easy enough as me apologising? Do I not have to worry about him anymore as long as I say "sorry"?

After we sign out of the hotel, he walks us back towards the underground station and we pop into a coffee shop for a muffin and a drink. I order a latte, grateful for the caffeine, and we're on our way again, tracing the steps from last night in a much happier way.

Even getting back on the train he's being all nice to me. Maybe he knows that Abbi messaged me and he's trying to be on his best behaviour to prove her wrong? I don't know. I need to stop assuming everything and just live in the moment. No matter what Abbi says later, I can deal with it... I think. I just don't *want* to; everything seems to be getting back on track for us now that we've had our hiccup, and I'm so terrified that she will tell me something that will mess it all up.

But right now, with him looking at me like that, I don't think there's anything that can rip this away from us.

I love this boy so much and he wants me... What more can I ask for?

Twenty One

A while later, the train pulls into my stop.

"I'll see you this weekend, yeah?" he says, pulling me in for a final kiss. "I'll be missing you like crazy until then."

"Same here!" I say. I think I mean it; I don't know what's going to happen with Abbi later and I also can't know for certain if Ash will ever find out that I'm going behind his back. But it could all be fine, so why worry? I've wanted him to be my boyfriend again for so long, to prove to him that I made mistakes before but I can be a better girlfriend now that I know that.

And maybe Abbi is trying to ruin it all, just like she did when she first stole Ash from me.

"See you later!" I say, running from the carriage just as the doors open. The morning air hits me hard, waking me up to the day, and I watch Ash through the window as the train takes him away from me. The last twenty-four hours feel like such a haze; so much has happened and none of it seems simple. But I can work it all out this afternoon. In the meantime, I have to go and find Zoe so she can keep me motivated to finish this damn essay.

I walk back through campus and head to my dorm. As soon as I close the front door, I'm hounded by Zoe, Megan and Kelsey… and Michael?

"Uhm, hey guys," I say, feeling a little overwhelmed at the welcome.

"Girlie!" Megan says, with almost a serious tone. "You have some explaining to do."

"Can it wait until after my essay is finished? Just give me a few hours," I say. But then I remember: "Oh, it will have to be a quick update because I'm seeing Abbi this afternoon."

"YOU ARE WHAT!?" Megan says. I don't think I've ever seen her look so absolutely astounded before.

"Yes, so I really need to get a move on," I laugh. Something tells me in my gut that this will be a lot easier to deal with if I just turn it into a humorous situation, then I can't take it too seriously and I'll be able to focus long enough to reach the minimum word count.

"Ugh, fine," Megan says with a huff. "But you finish it as quickly as you can, submit that silly thing, and come find us." She links arms with Kelsey and the two head off down the corridor, Michael following after them. Zoe and I are left all alone.

"Are you okay?" she asks in a whisper. I guess all the excitement of the news has worn off and she's now realised how stressful today actually is for me.

"I don't know yet," I admit. "But I've promised myself I won't think about it until after my essay is done. I don't want Ash to affect my grade anymore

210

than he probably already has. And, Zoe, a lot happened last night..." I add this last bit almost reluctantly, but I know that I can't keep sugar-coating everything anymore. I have to start being honest with her, and maybe she can tell me *how* I messed up enough to make him behave like that. It will be easier with two of us figuring it out.

"Okay, well," she begins. "Good luck, yeah?"

"Thanks, Zoe," I say. I take a deep breath and smile; but who am I proving something to?

Zoe goes back to her room, and I do the same. It's strange to think that the last time I was in here, I was a very different Harper. I didn't know where Ash and I stood, or what he was going to say about getting back together properly. But I had all these high hopes of how he would ask me to be his girlfriend again; they were shattered, but he took me to London! That's something I can't forget about; I have to remember how he did that for me.

Before I start anything, I change into some fresh clothes and tie my hair back into a ponytail. It will make it a lot easier to work if I can't smell yesterday on me.

But when I open up the laptop and stare at the last paragraph I wrote, I have no idea how to continue. Why did I even pick this essay in the first place? It's probably the hardest one on there!

It doesn't matter, though, because I have no choice but to carry on.

211

And so I write. I write about how Austen depicts the women in her books, how they are always connected to a man in some way as though it is inevitable that they will end up together. It's almost like they can't exist by themselves; no matter how many accomplishments they have, they still pine after a man eventually.

It reminds me of myself. I'm sat here in a university dorm, writing an essay for a topic I actually love, for a degree I've always wanted. But where does my mind keep wandering to? Ash. It always leads back to him.

But is that such a bad thing? He's my boyfriend…I love him…

I'm *supposed* to?

Right?

***

It takes the rest of the morning, but I'm able to submit a finished copy of the essay before the deadline at noon. It's absolutely terrifying pressing the 'submit' button; it's like I'm sealing my fate. But it's kind of exciting in a way because it's my first assignment! In an English student kind of perspective, it's symbolic of how everything is just beginning.

My degree… My friends… Ash.

And some things are ending too.

I promised Ash that I would never speak to Nick again and I'm going to try so hard to make sure that

212

it actually happens. Even in a group setting, I'll be dry and quiet with him until I can find my way out of the situation completely. Because I completely get where Ash is coming from. It makes me feel simply nauseous to think about him being with Abbi, about all the things that they've done, and I don't want him to ever feel that way.

I knock on Zoe's door; I want to tell her everything first before the other girls. To be honest, I'm not even sure if I want to tell them *all* the things that happened. I might just give them the plastered-over version later.

"You finished it?" she says, opening it up and letting me come in.

"Don't sound so shocked," I joke, though I don't have much energy left in me for humour; the last few hours have been draining. I sit down on her bed and put one of her decorative pillows on my lap; what I have to tell her won't be easy by any means and I need all the comfort I can get. She closes the door behind us and joins me.

"Right, tell me everything," she says. There is so much concern on her face in this moment that I know she cares about me; she would do anything to make sure that I'm okay and I feel safe to tell her. So I do. I explain last night in detail, even explaining about how he grabbed onto my wrist and pulled me down the street, how he paid for our meal with my card, passing it as his own. How he became so much nicer as soon as I apologised.

213

"But the problem is, I don't really know how to *keep* him happy," I conclude. "I think there's something wrong me. And I have to meet Abbi in a few hours; who knows what she's going to say?"

"Well, that was a lot," Zoe says, her eyes widening as though her brain is resetting. "Firstly, are you okay?"

"Yes, I'm fine!" I insist; I think it's true. "I just need you to tell me what to do."

"I can't do that, Harper," she says slowly. "You chose Ash, you let him come back, and you love him."

"Yeah," I say, not sure where she's going with this.

"But what you've just told me doesn't sound great..."

"Yeah, that's what I'm saying!" I jump in, glad that she understands. "I did something wrong and I *keep* doing something wrong. But what is it?! Why am I not enough for him?" The words keep coming out of me and I realise there's actually so much I want to say and ask.

"Harper, slow down!" Zoe says, holding onto my arms to steady me on the bed. "You are not the problem."

"What?"

I don't know what she means or why she's saying that.

"I'm clearly the issue, Zoe! If I wasn't, he wouldn't keep getting angry, or disappearing, or leaving me

214

for other people! He wouldn't be all hot and cold and good and then bad and absolutely perfect but not want me! Don't you get it? I'm the one who keeps messing everything up; I've never had a boyfriend before Ash and I don't know what I'm doing, but I don't know how to fix it. I *need* to fix it."

"You don't need to do anything," she says. She's so calm with her words that she makes me look absolutely loony. Maybe I am. It would explain why Ash never wants me until I'm sorry for something I don't even know I've done.

"Please help me, Zoe," I say. And now I'm crying; there's actually full-on tears brimming in my eyes. They're probably all the ones I held in last night and all the ones I've been trying to suppress about meeting Abbi. But the truth is, this is too much.

"Harper, I think you need to hear Abbi out later," she begins and I know that whatever she says, she means it from the bottom of her heart. I can just tell by the tone she's saying it in. "But if she tells you something bad about him, about something that he's done, you have to at least consider that it's true."

"But what if it's something I don't want to hear?" I ask. "That's what I'm scared of. I can't pretend if it's out there, existing physically. I know that I'm not perfect but I can work on that, but if I find out that Ash has done something to or with her, then I don't know how to take that. I stopped talking to Nick when he asked me to."

"Yeah, he did tell us…" she says awkwardly.

215

"Oh my god, does he hate me?" I ask, squinting my eyebrows in concern. He was so lovely to me; I don't want to think about him being all hurt because of me.

"No, he's way too good of a man to be petty like that," she says comfortingly. "But Ash, on the other hand, is different."

"I know he's different! That's why I want to be with him" I tell her again. Why doesn't she get it?

"I understand," she says. "Just, don't think too much about it until you talk to Abbi. Do you want me to come with you?"

"No, it's okay," I reply, making up my mind. "I think this is something I have to do by myself. But, I would not say no to a bit of spying."

"Spying?!" she asks, practically bursting backwards. "What on earth do you mean by that?"

"You don't have to be sat with us…" I say, holding my hands up in innocence. "I'm just throwing it out there… I'm not telling you to do anything. But seriously, it might actually be helpful to know that you guys are around, just in case."

"Done," she says quickly. "You are not alone in this. Just, promise me you will actually listen to what she says and not just get defensive? And also, don't throw coffee down her front or anything crazy."

"I will try, is that good enough? And no promises on the second thing!"

Twenty Two

As I walk up to the coffee shop, I find myself already searching for any sign of Abbi through the glass. I don't know why I bother; it's so reflective that it's hard to make anything out. But it's all that's on my mind. Though, what does help is knowing that my friends are already sat in there at their own table. We didn't want to make it too obvious that they are there with me by walking in together, so this way it's more inconspicuous.

Zoe filled Megan and Kelsey in for me. I just couldn't go through it all again and I needed time to calm myself down and think about what I want to say to Abbi. Technically, I don't think that I need to say anything at all; she's the one who wants to explain things to me. But I feel like this could be a good opportunity to maybe get things off my chest.

I push forward on the door, taking a subtle breath so that I don't look like an idiot as much I feel. I scan the room slowly, spotting the girls in a back corner. It's a good table to choose; you can see pretty much the whole room. But there, at the table by the door, is Abbi.

It's weird seeing her in person.

217

I still remember the first time I saw her Instagram when I caught Ash scrolling it once. Even at the time, I couldn't deny that she was beautiful, but it just made me all the more jealous of how she had his attention. I was the girlfriend, but somehow I was put on the sidelines for some girl he had only just met.

And then she surpassed me. In Ash's eyes, this girl in front of me was better.

She's stunning, I get that much. But why did he choose her over me and what we had together? It's all becoming a little too real now, seeing her there in the flesh, that tears start to prick in my eyes. I can't help myself, but I can hold it in enough so that I don't have a full on breakdown in a coffee shop.

Abbi notices how I'm hovering awkwardly in the doorway and stands up to greet me properly. But she too must realise how strange this is because, once she's up, she slows down and hesitates.

"Hey," she says. "Thanks for coming. I know it must have been hard."

"No problem."

MASSIVE PROBLEM. I can't do this?! Why did I think that I could do this!?

Ash is going to be so annoyed at me when he finds out, because he probably will. And once again I'll have shown him that I'm a terrible girlfriend; I can't even trust him.

"Do you want to order first? I already got mine," she asks.

218

"Yeah, give me a minute," I tell her. I'm almost grateful that she has given me an excuse to walk away for a moment so that I can process this. It's so odd. So, so, odd. There's no queue so I'm served quickly, and I collect my latte annoyingly swiftly. When I return to the table she's sat down again, sipping on her own cup.

"What did you get?" she asks.

"We don't have to do the small talk," I say, maybe a little too bluntly. But it hurts, okay? She literally had sex with my boyfriend when she knew that I existed and she probably doesn't even care.

"Okay," she breathes. "Look, as I said in my text, I don't know how much Ash has told you. But I really don't think it will be the truth."

"Right, and what *is* the truth?" My question comes out confidently but I'm far from it. Not only is she a crap person, but Abbi is also sat on the wrong side of the table for me to see my friends for support. They're behind me and I have no clue if they're watching all of this, if they can hear it.

"I broke up with Ash," she says bluntly.

"What?" I say, confused. "That's not what *he* said."

"Yeah, I thought he might have twisted it to suit him," she says, rolling her eyes. "Harper, I'm not the bad guy here. I was just a bit stupid; he's really manipulative."

There's that word again, the one that Zoe always liked to bring up whenever we spoke about him.

219

"He's not that bad," I say. There's no way I'm letting her talk rubbish about him behind his back.

"No, that's the thing," she says, this time more seriously. "I didn't realise at first because I fell for it. And you're clearly still falling for it now. Before you come for me, I know how much you love him. And I know that he loves you."

"Of course he does," I reply. I don't know why she's saying it like that, as though it's wrong.

"But the way that he loves isn't healthy," she carries on. I don't want to hear it; all these words are just echoes of what Zoe used to say. But for some reason, I do listen. Because one little part of me wonders... one part of me is thinking 'what if she's right?' "He's really good at convincing people, of wrapping them around his finger. And he was able to do that because neither of us like ourselves much."

"I *do* like myself," I say, perhaps a little too quickly.

"If you did, then you wouldn't have torn yourself apart for him," she says simply. "I did it too, for a while. But I knew he was still talking to you."

Over the last few weeks, I have wondered how much she knew. But I was too busy thinking about myself to really care about how she was feeling. Besides, she took him from me first. She's the bad person here.

"It made me realise how you might have felt when you were together," she says. "I took him from you, yes, but he *left* you. And, I have to be honest,

220

Ash and I did have sex while you guys were together."

There it is, just like a slap to the face.

I always knew in the back of my mind that it had probably happened; I just didn't want to believe that it could have. But now I have certainty… and a mental image.

"He said you were having problems; that you were crazy," she goes on, and I'm still in so much shock that I can't say a thing. "He said that he was going to break up with you, he was just waiting to do it at the right time so that he didn't hurt you. And I didn't realise it at the time, because I'm literally eighteen and stupid, but just by being with me he had already hurt you. And I am so sorry that I did that to you. I know there isn't an excuse, but it wasn't *just* my fault. Ash is really dangerous; he is so clever with his words and putting you down so that he can be the one to pick you back up again."

"What are you saying?"

"I'm *saying*," she says, taking a breath. "Ash isn't a good boyfriend. I broke up with him because he's bad for me; he made me an awful person, for one. But, after a while, he became so inconsistent with me. He started disappearing, only for a few hours at first… but then for days at a time. He just refused to acknowledge me. So I complained. But doing that just riles him up, because it's not part of his plan. If you call him out, it just makes him angry. And I didn't want

221

to keep being silenced over something that I was completely allowed to be mad about."

Hearing her say all of this… it's exactly the same as how he is with me. But that doesn't mean that the situations are the same; after all, he came back to *me*. He chose *me*.

"And then I noticed he started going on his phone a lot more when he was around me," she says. This part looks hard for her to get out. "I didn't know it was you at first."

"How did you find out?" I ask. I have to know it all, now that we've started; it's addictive. And, even though my breathing hasn't been steady for the last few minutes, I know that I have no choice other than to hear her out. I have to know all the facts and make my choice, just like Zoe said.

"A few days ago, he came to mine after work," she begins. Her face looks terrified as she pictures it; what on earth could have happened to make her look *so* scared? "He wasn't in a good mood at all, and apparently it was my job to fix that… by doing whatever he wanted."

It's all starting to sound too familiar now. Sickeningly familiar.

"And I let him."

Okay, *really* familiar.

"But it wasn't *my* name that he was calling out."

"What?" I ask. I heard her, but I didn't expect her to say that. "He was thinking about *me*?"

222

"Don't look so happy," she says. "He was thinking about you because you were easier to use. He was getting bored of me, annoyed at how I wasn't going to settle for the bare minimum. I was so up and down with what and when I accepted his crappy behaviours that it was just making me really hate who I was with him. So I ended things. And then I saw on snap maps that he was at yours, and I just knew."

"In the exact same way I did," I say. It doesn't come out in a petty way, not even in an angry sort of tone. It's just an understanding, one that was created between us by the same boy.

"Yeah," she says. "I really needed you to know that he was horrible to me, and I know that he was the same with you. He probably still is, isn't he? And you're just excusing it because you love him and every part of you wants him to be better. You don't want to accept the fact that he can't do that, at least not until he realises that what he's doing is wrong. And that is probably going to take him a really long time. Do you see what I mean?"

"No," I say. This isn't something I need to think about. Everything that she is saying is utter rubbish, stemming from her jealousy at the situation. "There's nothing wrong with Ash; it's you that the problem."

"I know I didn't do a good thing," she begins to say. But I'm past caring now; I don't have to sit here and listen to her tearing my boyfriend down. For all I know, she's lying about her doing the breaking off. I

223

will ask Ash, though, because he can confirm my doubts for me.

"I honestly don't want to hear what you have to say anymore," I tell her bluntly. My eyes are wide open in an attempt not to cry or panic; I just hope she can't see through me.

"I know it's hard, but –"

"You don't get a fucking say," I tell her. "You took Ash from me and that broke me. Okay? I don't want to feel like that again just because you want him back."

"I do not want him back," she says, throwing her hands up to feign innocence.

"I'm not stupid," I say.

"No, just naive," she comments.

"You don't know me," I reply dryly.

"I know Ash."

She's looking at me shamelessly, her eyes burning into me. I promised Zoe that I would hear her out and I've done that enough now. I just want to leave this damn coffee shop and go and see Ash; he can tell me that everything is okay and she's talking absolute crap.

"I'm going," I say. "Thanks for nothing."

Without looking back, I storm from the coffee shop, letting the door slam behind me. I'm only a few meters away when the girls catch up to me, enveloping me in a huddle.

And I cry.

Outside this stupid coffee shop, I cry.

I cry for Ash. I cry for Abbi. I cry for me.

And I cry for all the girls that have had to go through the same thing as me. It hurts too bad knowing where else his lips were once, when they should have only been on mine.

Twenty Three

The girls walk me to the train station, trailing beside me like they're scared to leave. They offer to come with me but I don't need them there. Why would I? I'm only going to spend some time with Ash after I had to rush away from him this morning. Besides, I have to prove Abbi wrong. I have to show her that he does love me, that he does want me, and that we are happy together.

I don't exactly know how I'll tell her that because I don't plan on talking to her ever again. But she will know that I didn't leave him. She might see it on his social media, or notice us walking about town one day. She can be jealous all she wants; I'm not letting her take him from me again.

"Are you sure you're going to be okay?" Zoe asks as we walk up to the ticket barriers.

"Why wouldn't I be?" I question.

"Because you've cried the entire walk over here," Megan scoffs.

I wipe away my tears with my sleeve and put on a stronger face.

"Abbi just made me uncomfortable," I say. "I'm allowed to hate her after what she did to me.

Besides, she was talking rubbish about Ash. None of it was true!"

"She's going to have her own experiences with him," Zoe says. "They might be different to yours, but maybe you should listen to her... she might be right about him."

"Oh and you'd love that, wouldn't you?" I say. "You all hate him. I know it. You've tried to pretend that you were happy with us getting back together but you're not at all. You just kept quiet because I asked you to. But I *love* him and he loves me. I'm not giving up on that. I can't."

"Call us if you do need us," Kelsey says. "But I hope you have a good time tonight."

"Thank you," I say. Then, I add snarkily: "At least one of you gets it."

And I scan my newly-bought ticket and walk over to the platform. It feels right to be so tunnel vision on him again. Last night was a fluke; he didn't mean to hurt me and I was a complete ass of a girlfriend. But we're not always bad. Sometimes we're beautiful. And I'm going to show everyone.

Heading onto the train reminds me of last night. That amazing man made one of my longest dreams come true by taking me to London and I threw it back in his face, worrying about an essay that I really should have finished ages ago. He wasn't wrong at all; I was just panicked, blaming him.

I'm hopeful that seeing him this evening will help him realise how much he means to me.

But as the train nears my town, a little bit of sick buckles at the back of my throat. I remember what Abbi had said in the coffee shop, about how she was the one who broke up with him... how he might be talking to someone else already.

I try to bat it away as I step onto the platform. It's already dark outside and I'm not really surprised; it is February, after all.

But it makes the short trek to his house even worse. The streets feel empty and dangerous, even though I know that there is rarely any crime here. The thing we have to worry about the most is if a mobility scooter decides to run out of battery while crossing the street.

Yet, my heart isn't steady.

I don't know why I haven't messaged him yet to check if he's even at home. Part of me really wants it to be a surprise. I've always hated them because I like to know what is happening, otherwise it makes me anxious. But Ash likes things like that. They make him feel special.

As I reach his street, a wave of familiarity washes over me, caressing me. The two of us had spent our whole summer hanging out in his bedroom, basking in the privacy it gave us.

The living room light is on. We never really hung out in there because his parents work from home. There was always the risk of someone coming in and seeing us; even I could agree that it was better to hide away upstairs.

But as I begin to walk up the front path, it's not his parents that I'm seeing in the living room.

No.

There are two people in there, though.

Only, it's Ash.

And a girl.

I falter backwards, not sure of what to do.

Am I supposed to bang on the window? Show him that I know?

Do I call his number and see what he says? See if he lies?

Yes, that's a good idea.

I head back onto the main street and stand on the other side. I'll be hidden by the darkness but Ash's body is clear as day as he presses it against yet another girl who isn't me.

Bringing up his number takes no time at all, but finding the courage to dial it is difficult.

As it rings through, I worry that he won't even answer it at all. But he pauses his make-out session to look down at what I assume is the coffee table based on the last time I was there.

They are no longer kissing... that's good, at least.

"Hey?" His voice is like charcoal down the line and I don't want to burn.

"Hi," I say but it comes out in a wrinkled quiver.

"So, what's up?" he questions, clearly not wanting to stay on the call.

I have to hold it together. I can't lash out. If he realises that I'm outside of his house right now, he will think I'm crazy. He will say that I'm stalking him and that I can't possibly be a good girlfriend because I don't even trust him.

And oh my god...

Abbi was right.

Everything she said back in the coffee shop was real, I just didn't want to believe it.

How stupid can I be? He already cheated on me once with Abbi and he didn't even hesitate to have another lined up. I'm nothing to him.

No, that's unfair. I am something: I'm replaceable.

"I was just wondering what you're up to," I say. He doesn't reply, but he does look at her. "We could call for a bit, if you're free."

"Yeah," he says, still looking at her. He moves the phone away from his ear and covers the mic with his hand to tell her something. I'm too far away to read his lips, yet she's close enough to kiss them. "Now's not a good time."

"Oh, how come?" I ask, begging him to just be honest with me.

"Got an extra shift at work," he says. His words come out easily, as though lying to me is nothing. "I'm not even at home; I already left."

"Right," I say, stifling my tears. "Another time, then."

"Definitely," he says. "Love you."

"I lo -"

The line dies.

He throws the phone down and then throws *himself* onto her body again. Frozen, I watch them for a few minutes. But my eyes aren't really looking at what they're doing; I'm too busy thinking about everything that's happened to really notice anymore.

Everyone said it was bad, but I don't think they meant *this* bad. And now I'm going to have to do something about it, because I can't stay with him now, can I?

I suppose I can. I could try and see him tomorrow and never mention what I've seen today. Things will carry on as normal and I'll keep trying to be a better girlfriend for him.

But maybe I'm not enough.

Or perhaps I'm just not enough for him. And maybe I never will be.

Eventually, I turn and walk away from his street. At first, I don't know where to go, but I don't want to go back to uni. There is no way I can sit on a train and not hold my tears in. People will be looking at me with concern and I don't want to have to explain to strangers that the boyfriend who has already cheated on me has literally done it again. I'll be the stupid one, then.

I should have never let him come back.

I just want him so badly.

I want to be loved.

But this isn't love.

No, it's far from it.

232

Twenty Four

Since I can't go back to campus, there is only one other place for me to head to: home.

I haven't been there in ages; I think the last time was over the Christmas holidays, and even then I wasn't emotionally anywhere. Ash had only just broken up with me at that point and every day felt like a chore, a punishment for scaring him away.

Taking the usual path to my house from Ash's feels more painful than I ever thought it would. I know every turn and road like the back of my hand, yet it feels different this time. We're still technically together... girlfriend and boyfriend... Harper and Ash. But we're also not. Not really.

Ash has cheated on me for the second time now, maybe even more and I just haven't found out about them. I don't think you can do that to someone you love... I know I couldn't.

What I had with Nick was different. I was single at that point, but even then I felt guilty as though I was betraying Ash and what we had. No, with me, there was never any overlap.

To reach my house, I choose to walk along the seafront, hopeful that the fresh air will help to clear my mind and calm me down. I can imagine all the times I spent with Ash here easily, but I try not to think about them too deeply. I've managed to hold back my tears so far; I can't start now.

The waves crash against the wall, sending little splashes of water against my coat. I don't care, though. At least I can feel *something*; I don't want to be numb again.

I stand here for a moment, watching nothing in particular, and bask in it all. I have never wanted to accept a life without Ash in it, even when it hurts to have him around. But now? Everything has changed. No matter how mad I was at Abbi earlier on, I realise now that she was right. She may not be the most amazing person, but all she did was fall for the same lies I did. If she's bad, I am too.

I should probably speak to her at some point and apologise for storming off, but I don't think I could do that in a way that isn't spiteful yet.

No, for now I need to focus on how I'm going to get past this... how I'm going to break up with him.

God, that feels so wrong to say. If I thought kissing Nick was a betrayal, this is like stabbing his heart with a knife and twisting it, splattering his blood across my face.

I wipe away a tear with my sleeve and turn from the sea, climbing up the steps to my street. When I was younger, I always used to love living here, where I could look out of my bedroom window and see the beach. Now, it feels like hell.

That was our beach. Mine and Ash's.

And all that's left are tainted memories.

As I reach my house, I realise that I don't have my keys on me. Instead, I knock on the door, grateful to see lights on.

"Harper?" mum says, opening the door with a confused face.

"Can I stay tonight?" I say and then all the tears I've been saving stream down my cheeks.

"Yes, yes, of course!" she says, opening the door wider for me to come in. She strokes my back comfortingly as I walk past her. "You don't have anything with you?"

I shake my head.

"Okay, not to worry," she says, thinking. "You've still got some clothes here and you're bed is all made. I'll get you a new toothbrush out of the cupboard and -"

"Ash cheated on me," I cry.

"Oh, Harper!" she says, pulling me in for a hug. My tears fall onto her t-shirt, staining a pool of water against the red of the fabric...

Red was his favourite colour.

"What can I do to help?" she says.

"I don't know," I moan. "I don't know."

"Do you want your friends over?" she asks and I take a few seconds to think about them all.

I treated them so horribly before I left. All I could think about was seeing Ash and making everything right between us again, proving Abbi wrong. And in

235

the meantime, I hurt my closest friends... the people who have been there for me through all of this mess... the people who stood by my side even when I insisted on being with him.

"Maybe tomorrow," I say. Tonight, I don't want to explain what I saw to anyone. I need time to think about it all, to process what happened and what I'm going to do about it... how I'm going to walk away from the person I love the most.

"Of course," she says. "Have you eaten? Do you need some food?"

"Don't you have to go to work tonight?" I ask. She always works the night shift when she can to earn extra money; it's rare for her to have a night off.

"I'll call in sick," she says without hesitating.

"No, don't do that," I reply. "Honestly, I'll be fine."

"I'm not leaving you here by yourself like this," she answers. "Give me a minute to let my manager know."

There isn't any point trying to argue with her so as she heads into the kitchen, I walk like a ghost into the living room. There are memories with Ash here too, but not so many. Since my mum was always at home during the day, he was never a fan of hanging out here, not when his room was more private.

But this is better than my uni room... the place where he'd once been so many times. At least here, there was a time before him.

That scuff on the wall... I'd accidently thrown a ball at it when I was little.

The stain on the carpet... I'd spilt my drink during a sleepover.

There are a lot of memories here. Some are happy and some I wish I hadn't lived, but at least they don't belong to him too. It makes it easier to bear.

"Right, let's get some food," she says, coming into the living room. "Do you fancy lasagne?"

I used to love it as a kid. She'd make it all the time for me when I was upset... Now seems like a perfectly suitable time for her to offer it again.

"Sounds good," I say. I'll probably struggle to eat anything right now; there's no point being picky.

"Perfect!" she says, but I feel far from it.

She's trying to be all smiley and happy, hoping that it will help me feel better. But I just feel like an idiot for giving him a second chance. I feel even more stupid for blaming myself. I never *told* him to cheat on me twice... I never *told* him to hurt me...

I never *told* him to use my body like it's worthless.

No, he did that. He did everything and I sucked it up and took it because I don't love myself. Abbi knows that; she did it too. But she was smart enough to figure it out and do something about it.

And me?

I went running straight back to him.

But I won't anymore. I'm done chasing someone who doesn't deserve me. Because I am Harper and I *can* exist without him.

***

I wake up in the morning with puffy eyes. I cried so much last night that it felt like I'd never stop... and I don't think I did. As I fell into sleep, my heart was still bleeding from it all.

I don't feel any better this morning. All of me wants to rot in bed, to curl up with my childhood teddies and just let the days go by... never having to deal with it. But I can't do that again. Not to myself. And not because of Ash.

I prise my body from my sheets and tiptoe down the stairs quietly. I don't know what to expect as I haven't been home in so long, but I'm shocked to see mum standing over the hob making pancakes.

"Hi," I say softly, hovering by the door.

"Oh, good morning!" she says, smiling at me in the same pitiful way she had last night. "I'm making your favourite!"

"I can see," I say. "Thanks."

"No worries," she adds, placing one of them onto a place on the island. I tiptoe over and take a seat on one of the stools. "Are you going to invite the girls over today?"

"Yeah," I say. "I'll see if we can meet up in town, though. There's something I need to do."

238

"Oh, yeah?" she says curiously.

"I'm going to break up with Ash," I say, the words feeling like poison. "I think I have to."

"I didn't even know you were back together..." she says and I realise how much I've left her out of all of this. I just always assumed she wouldn't want to hear about him; she wasn't exactly his biggest fan.

"I guess it just slipped my mind," I say. "It's not been very long."

"You can tell me anything, you know that, right?" she says.

"Yeah, of course," I lie. She would never have been able to support me in my decision to let Ash back in, mainly because it was a terrible idea. But it wouldn't have been her place to say. She may have my best interests at heart, but she can't speak for me. She can't make my decisions. I'm only eighteen; I need to make my own mistakes.

"Good," she replies. "Now, eat up and then you can text your friends."

Twenty Five

After breakfast, I drop everyone a text in the flat group chat and they reply instantly, telling me that they will be on the next train. It's a relief, that's for sure, because it means they can't be *too* mad at me. I just hope that they will all forgive me when I explain.

I get myself ready, changing into some clothes I'd left behind when I'd travelled back to uni at the beginning of January. I've opted for a pair of baggy blue jeans and a purple sweatshirt. It's a comfy enough outfit and will match the coat I have here so I won't be overly cold when we go out.

Worried about looking a complete mess and it being obvious that I've been crying all night, I do apply a bit of makeup. Just a touch of mascara and blush to hide how I'm feeling. It will be enough to fool Ash; he never looks too deeply at me, anyway.

All I can do for now is think about how my friends will be here soon, ready to help me through this absolute disaster I've got myself into.

***

When I reach the station, the girls are already there waiting for me. I walk up to them awkwardly, hands in my pocket.

"How are you?" Zoe asks, concern flooding her face.

"Not great... I'm really sorry about last night, guys," I say. "I was so mad at the things Abbi was saying, partly because I think I knew she was right even then. I went to Ash's last night..."

"What happened?" Megan asks.

"He was kissing another girl," I say, replaying it all in my head... their hands on each other's bodies, their lips and tongues dancing together.

"Not even Abbi?" Megan scoffs. "What a dickhead!"

"Totally," Zoe says. "And don't worry about yesterday; we all completely understand."

"Thanks," I whisper. "And thank you for coming round."

"Of course!" Kelsey says, giving me a supportive smile.

"What did you need us for? Retail therapy?" Megan asks, as though her hands are already on the cash in her pocket. She loves shopping.

"I'm going to breakup with Ash today," I admit.

"You're what!?" Megan squeals. "Oh my god, I have never been more proud of you!"

"Megan," Zoe glares at her. "This isn't going to be easy for her at all. We can celebrate when she's ready."

"Yes, sorry," Megan adds.

"It's okay," I reply. "I'm going to ask him to meet me soon."

"You ready to text him now?" Megan asks.

"I have no idea how to do this," I tell her. "My hands are shaking so much that it's going to take me all day to get it out."

"You've got this," Zoe says.

We're all now huddled in a little group outside the train station. I hate being back in *my* hometown and it feeling like it belongs to Ash. It seems completely unfair that I'm going to have to walk around worried to bump into him whenever I come back from uni. How will I even react? Will I say hi, wave, run in the completely opposite direction? No, I need to stop thinking about this. Like Zoe said, my only focus is on ending things; I need to be as tunnel vision on him as I usually am, even if the circumstances are slightly different.

I open up our messages and begin to type, hoping that he will see it quickly and not use this as one of his times to disappear.

> hey, I'm back home.
> could we meet
> somewhere now?

I stare at the screen nervously, and, thankfully, he opens it straight away. The three little dots dance about until his message finally comes through.

you're here??

He sounds mainly confused but also a little scared; there's a little niggle in my gut, wondering what he's up to right now. He's probably still with her; the girl from last night.

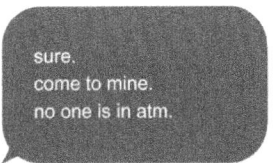

sure.
come to mine.
no one is in atm.

"Oh my gosh, Harper," Megan groans, noticing how much I'm mitigating it. "Do this on your terms. It doesn't matter if he would rather you come to his house so he can bone you."

"I don't want to make him feel forced," I say. "And don't say 'bone', it sounds weird."

"Yeah, but you do know why he wants you to come to his house, don't you?" she says. "It would just be a repeat of the other night."

"I know," I reply, trying really hard not to think about the specifics.

sure, josie's in 30 mins?

works for me!

It feels brutal not to tell him, to pretend like we are simply hanging out because we are in a relationship and I want to see him. But right now, I don't want to see him at all, because I know that when I do, I'm going to have to break his heart like he broke mine. And the thing is, none of this even makes complete sense yet; I'm still seeing both sides of the argument and it's like I'm torn between them. Staying means that he will keep making me do things that I don't want to do. I'll have to always be worrying about who he's talking to or when he might just randomly disappear for a few days. I'd be risking my peace for someone that doesn't actually want me.

If he *really* wants me, he wouldn't have cheated on me with Abbi or this new girl. He wouldn't have lied to me about the fact that she was the one who broke up with him. Instead, he twisted the narrative to fit his lies; he went with the option that had the biggest outcome of me letting him back in. And in my naivety and blind love for him, I fell for it. But I wanted so badly to believe that he could be a good person… that he was *my* person. But I don't think he can change and I don't like who I'm becoming just so that I can be with him.

"We've got half an hour," I tell everyone. "He's going to meet me at Josie's. He took me there on a date once."

I don't actually know why I say it. Maybe because it's what comes to my brain and I know that there's only so much longer I can talk about him to people. Well, I guess I'll still *talk* about him, but it won't be in the same way; it won't be in the "my boyfriend…" sense anymore.

"What do you want to do while we wait?" Zoe asks me.

"I don't know," I say. "Find a bin to be sick in?" I try to joke to make it seem like I'm doing okay, but they're all looking at me like I need serious help and I both hate and love it at the same time. I appreciate them all being here, giving me support, but I don't like how they're all pitying me because I was stupid enough to fall for someone who's low-key abusive.

Woah. No, that word is way too harsh for what this is. Or, at least, I think it is. But if it isn't that, what *is* it?

"We could do some shopping? Buy some self-care things to make tonight easier?" Kelsey suggests.

"Yeah, we could do that," I say. I think I can manage it; maybe it will be a nice distraction walking around the familiar shops with my friends. All I can say is that I wish it was in nicer circumstances, where I

246

could show them all my favourite places and point out spots where I had beautiful memories.

The only problem is, I'm already looking at all the places that are tainted with Ash like little mourning places dotted about.

There's the bench where we sat and people-watched because we'd ran out of things to talk about...

And there's the store we went to when we bought condoms together for the first time...

And there's the street that leads to his house.

As we walk through town, I try my best to keep it together. Each breath is practically forced so that I can keep my heart-beat calm enough not to fall into a panic attack over something that hasn't even happened yet. We head into a few smaller shops to glance at things on the shelves and then come out of Superdrug with a small bag of face masks and skincare products.

"You cannot let your skincare go just because you won't have a boyfriend anymore," Megan insists. It's a little harsh, but I get what she's saying. I remember when he first left; I'd developed spots within days and just never really bothered to try to get rid of them. It didn't seem important until he was on the verge of coming back to me, to us. From that point, I'd started it up again, applying creams and moisturizers daily so that I would stay pretty enough for him not to leave again. And now look at me: I'm the one walking away.

"We should probably start heading towards Josie's," Kelsey suggests. "Do you want us to come in with you? Or will it be too obvious?"

"I don't know," I say. "It's quite a small cafe; he would definitely recognise you all. I don't even know if he will be there before us and we definitely can't walk in together."

"We could hang about outside and watch through the window?" Zoe suggests.

"And what if it turns dirty?" Megan butts in. "Not in *that* way. But he's been physical with you before and he did it in front of people last night; I wouldn't put it past him if he gets annoyed with you."

"Okay, yeah, I can't do this," I say, reverting back to my fear. "He's gonna kill me."

"New plan," Zoe says. "We tell the staff members what's happening; just clue them in enough to keep an eye in case anything happens? And you can call someone so we can hear everything. If something is going to happen, we can come in straight away."

"Yeah, that might work," I say, thinking it through. It sounds like our best option by far; even it means telling someone else that Ash is a bad person. But honestly, I'm scared for my safety and no matter how much I love him, I really don't want him to hurt me like he did me last night. "Let's do that."

"Alright!" Megan says. I can tell by the way that she's talking that she's about to take charge. To be fair, as long as it's not me, I don't care who does. "Let's go there now and hope we get there before him. Otherwise, I don't even know what we are going to do."

"I'll ask if he's close," I say, dropping him a message. Oddly, he replies straight away:

running late.
don't think i'll be too
long though.

"He's late," I tell them.

"No surprise there, right?" Zoe says, smiling at me sympathetically.

"I guess not," I say. The likelihood of him being with another girl feels higher now, but it could be because of a number of reasons that don't involve a member of the opposite sex.

So, the four of us head to Josie's; it's only one next street over so it doesn't take too long. The cafe is small, squished into a row of terraced buildings that make up the main street in our town. But this always made it cosy to me; a little place of beauty hidden among the larger shops.

"Who's going in?" I ask. It doesn't make sense for all of us to go in and then walk back out.

"Who do you want to?" Kelsey asks. I think about it, but really I don't need to, because the choice is blatantly obvious.

"Zoe? Would you tell them with me?" I ask her.

"Of course I will!" she says, squeezing my hand.

"We'll hang about in that shop over there until we see Ash go in," Megan explains. "Then we'll come and watch from outside in the least suspicious way possible."

"Thanks," I say.

As they head to the shop, Zoe and I turn and walk into Josie's. She takes the lead, going straight to the counter. It's littered with plant pots and I'm jealous that they're able to keep them alive; I'm yet to be a successful succulent mum.

"Hey there!" the waitress says. She looks overly happy, as though working in a café is all she's ever wanted to do. She's worked here for as long as I can remember and I find a small sense of comfort in knowing a familiar face will always be around. I sometimes find it difficult to order things in public; it's one of the more annoying ways my anxiety perks up. But her being here, with that large, beaming smile, always helps out. I'm even more grateful for it today. "What can I get you?"

"This is a bit weird," Zoe says, leaning in and speaking quietly. The waitress comes closer too, realising that something must be up. "But my friend is about to meet her boyfriend here. He's running late, though, so we're not sure when he's going to arrive. But she's breaking up with him."

"Right?" the waitress questions.

"He's got a bit of a history of being abusive," Zoe continues and I wince when the word comes out of her mouth. "Our other friends are going to watch from outside and I'm going to join them in a moment. We don't want him to see any of us and freak out. But she's going to call me so we can hear what's going on. But please could you keep an eye on the situation, make sure he doesn't try anything?"

"Of course," she says. "I am so sorry," she directs at me. And then, turning back to Zoe: "If it's okay, I'll alert the other staff members, just for safety purposes."

"Thank you so much," Zoe says. "Could she get a coffee, please? A latte?"

I find a small bit of reassurance knowing that Zoe knows me, that she's here for me, that everyone is, even these strangers who are simply working their shift.

"I'll be just outside, okay?" Zoe says after paying for my coffee and starting the call between our phones. She's so lovely I could cry all over again. I nod at her, unable to find my words.

As she walks away, I take a seat by the window, hoping that it will help to give the girls a clearer view.

And then I wait.

I wait because once again, he can't be counted on.

Twenty Six

About twenty minutes later, he finally turns up, rocking into the cafe like he's completely innocent and hasn't had me waiting for ages.

"Hello, beautiful!" he says, kissing me on the forehead before sitting down on the chair opposite mine. I've done a lot of that recently: sitting and talking to people about things I don't want to, things that hurt to even think about.

"Hey, thanks for meeting me," I say, clearing my throat and looking down at my coffee. I hate how much this is mirroring my conversation with Abbi earlier... only I'm on the other side of it now. "How has your morning been?" I ask; I'm not ready to do the hard bit yet; that can wait. For now, I can ease into it and see what kind of mood he is in.

Have I always thought like this? Wondering how he is going to act and then basing my own behaviour on that? Maybe it *has* been bad, at least a little bit...

"No problem," he says. "So, did you just want to hang out with your amazing boyfriend? I can't believe you didn't tell me you were coming home for a few days!"

"I'm not staying," I say. "I'm just here for today because I needed to talk to you."

"You're looking a little too serious right now for my liking," he replies, his face beginning to change from the smiling eyes he had worn only a moment before.

It's happening… he's going to get mad as soon as I come out with it and I can't avoid it. I try to glance towards the counter as subtly as I can to see if any of the staff members are watching. The woman who served me makes eye contact with me as she stands behind the till and I know that I'm not alone right now. If anyone should be scared, it's Ash. He's closed in right now; he can't do anything physical here, but he can still use his words.

"Harper, what the fuck is wrong with you? Why has your face gone all weird?"

"I just need to tell you something," I say, trying really hard to get the words out without backing out.

"Well, say it then," he orders. "I thought you just wanted to see me? That you wanted to hang out?"

"I do! No, I don't, uhm," I stumble. It's already falling apart; how am I this weak? *This* scared of a boy I'm supposed to love and feel safe with?

"Harper, can you just stop doing whatever you're doing?" he snaps quietly. "I was really excited to see you and now you're being all cryptic and it's making me uncomfortable."

I'm making *him* uncomfortable?! I'm the one who can't breathe properly right now. The one who had to tell staff members at a stupid cafe to make sure I'm safe. The one who decided to love a boy who is so incredibly bad for me and I was blind to it? And now look at what I've got myself into; he left me once, I should have let him stay gone. Nick would have been the better choice; he never would have made me feel like this, because he never did. No matter how many times we spoke, I was still always just happy to see him. And I fumbled it. For Ash.

"I'm going to go and get a drink," he says. "Can I borrow your card? I forgot mine."

I look at him, dead in the eye. I can't believe he's trying this again, as though I wouldn't have caught on by now. But I can't say that I don't have mine with a coffee cup sat before me. And I can't say no. I never can when it comes to him.

"Sure," I say, passing him my bank card.

"Thanks, babe," he replies as he takes it. He walks over to the counter and I throw my head into my hands. How on earth am I going to go through with this? I thought I loved him, that I wanted to be with him? Do I just not want that anymore? I don't have a clue, but what I know for certain is that love shouldn't feel like this. I don't want to be with someone who scares me, just so that I can have their attention. Because that's what this is, isn't it? Ash can't love me in any real capacity and I don't think he ever could, otherwise he wouldn't have been able to leave me for Abbi.

A minute or so later, he joins me at the table with his coffee. I don't even bother to ask what he got, I don't care; I have more important things to think about right now. Like how I have tell my abusive boyfriend that I don't want to be in a relationship with him anymore.

"Man, I'm so thirsty," he says, sipping his coffee as he leans back in his chair. Compared to before, he seems completely unphased now, almost as though he has forgotten how angry he had been with me. I'll take it; the calmer he is, the easier this will be.

"Ash," I say, trying again. He peers at me over the glass before placing it down on the table with a small thump. It's like a warning.

"Harper, oh my god, what?"

Okay, so maybe he's still in a mood.

"I can't be with you anymore."

I said it. I actually said it? Those words came out of *my* mouth?

"What the fuck?" he spits back, reminding me that this isn't over at all. No, this is just the beginning and it's about to get really messy.

"I'm really sorry!" I begin, trying to bandage it all up as quickly as I can.

"You're *sorry*? Harper, that's fucking meaningless," he replies. His eyes are shooting daggers at me right now and all I want to do is turn my head to make sure someone is watching, someone is realising. But I don't dare; I can't move an inch. "Don't you love me anymore?"

"Of course I do," I say, leaning forward in my eagerness to have him believe me. Because he *needs* to believe me; I don't know why, but it just feels important. "But we're not good for each other."

"What is that supposed to mean?" he asks. "We're great for each other, Harper. I literally took you to London; you've wanted to do that for years. And I even brought you back in time to do your essay, even though I really wanted to stay."

"I know..." I say. He's right; he did do those things and they were so lovely, but they're not the whole story. "But you weren't very nice to me when we were there."

"Oh my god," he says, shaking his head at me. "I can't believe you. I can't do anything right, can I? I'm not perfect, but I try so hard to please you."

"Do you?" I question him. "Do you actually care about my feelings? What I want?"

"Of course I do, don't be ridiculous," he says, waving it away like it's nothing. But it's not, and I'm not.

"No," I say, surprised at my own defiance. "No, I'm not being ridiculous. I spoke to Abbi today."

"You did what?" he says, his voice rising slightly. "What did she say?" he adds, slightly panicked.

"That she broke up with you," I tell him bluntly.

"Well, she's lying," he says, but his voice is wavering.

257

"I'd like to believe that, Ash," I say. "I *really* want to, you have no idea, but she isn't. Because she told me other stuff too and it's all adding up."

"You can't trust what she says," he warns me. "She's just jealous because I chose you."

"You shouldn't be in the situation where you have to pick between two girls, Ash," I explain. "You should never have cheated on me in the first place; you don't do that if you're in love with someone. Besides, I know you were with someone last night."

"Were you stalking me? Ugh, you know what, it doesn't matter because I didn't *mean* to," he says, as though that's an excuse; he just accidentally stumbled into another girl's pants. "Last night was a one-off; I needed to be close with someone... Anyways, it was really confusing for me back then. I liked both you and Abbi, but me and you just weren't really going anywhere because you were at uni, like we couldn't be in a proper relationship, you know?"

"No, I *don't* know," I say. "Because I didn't sleep with someone else just because I moved an hour away from you. And I also didn't have a one night stand because I was *horny*."

And there it is. It's like I've finally pleaded innocent to myself after all of this time because I've realised that I wasn't the problem. Or, at least, not completely. I may not have been the perfect girlfriend, but I was never horrible or mean or violent. I was just a little insecure in myself and there isn't anything wrong with that; the only way it becomes a

258

problem is when someone like Ash comes along and takes advantage of that.

And I went through that.

Abbi went through it.

And so many other girls will have.

But I really don't think it's my fault anymore, and I definitely don't think that I deserved any of it.

"That's just bull," he complains. "I'm trying to communicate with you here about how hard it was for me and all you can think about is yourself."

"You're not communicating," I say. "You're just talking down at me, expecting me to treat all of your words as law. I may have done that once upon a time, Ash, but I'm done. I want to *like* myself again!"

"You already do," he tells me. "You're just being all dramatic and honestly, you're making a scene. It's embarrassing."

"It's all true..." I say, not to him, but to me. Everything that Abbi tried to explain to me and all the times that Zoe warned me... it's true. He is a narcissist and it's obvious. How have I let this go on for so long?

But I know the answer.

Love.

And, more specifically, first love... If I can even call it that.

Ash is my first boyfriend, the first person to show any interest in me, and I thought that meant that we had something special. But I don't think it does anymore. All it means is that I don't know what I'm doing because I don't know what makes a good

259

relationship. Yet, I think I'm starting to see what *doesn't* and that just might be enough to help me get through this.

"I don't want to keep talking," I say, looking him in the eye as much as I can bear without crying. I have to be strong in this moment to prove something to him; to show him that I'm not as weak as he's been thinking. "So, just to clarify, we are over. For now. For good. Never again. And I don't want you to reach out to me."

I start to put on my jacket, avoiding his gaze for my own sake. I've said what I needed to say, now all I can do is walk away and find the girls outside; they will get me through this next bit and everything will be fine because it *has* to be.

"I didn't say it was over," Ash says, standing up to block my way; he's right by the door and there's no way past.

"Let me through, please," I say calmly.

"No," he says. "Why should I? So you can walk away from me? No, I want to keep talking because you've just let Abbi's lies get into your head, don't you see that? Talk to me!" He grabs my wrists as I try to push around him and it throws me right back to the other night, walking the streets of London like a dog on a leash… being guided to a hotel room where he could do whatever he wanted because we were behind closed doors. And it's too much; it's *all* too much.

"Please let me go," I say again, trying to hold in the tears in front of him. I have to wait until I'm out of his sight. Just a little bit longer. Nearly over.

The girls outside will have heard it on the phone; they will be listening, ready to help me afterwards. It makes me feel a little better but it's not good enough to get me through this moment; Ash doesn't care that I'm terrified of him at all.

"I said *no*!" He pushes me back and I land on my back in the middle of a coffee shop in my hometown, looking up at the boy I once thought I loved.

Twenty Seven

"You need to leave," a voice says and I realise it's the woman from the counter. She's looking at Ash so seriously that I'm surprised when he hesitates.

"She just fell," he states.

"I'm not blind," is her harsh reply. "Now, get out and don't come back; you're banned, you hear me?"

"Oh whatever," he spits. "Harper, this isn't finished."

Reluctantly, he spins and slams the door of the cafe behind him. I watch him walk away, further and further past the window until he's gone completely.

"Here, love," the woman says, holding out her hand to help me up.

"Thank you," I say, wiping away a tear with the back of my hand. "I'm really sorry about that."

"Don't you apologise at all, darling!" she says, utterly shocked that I've even tried to take the blame. "You've got our support here; you come as much as you need; he won't be allowed past that door ever again."

"Thank you," I sniffle. "He didn't mean to push me. He was just a bit angry with me because I broke up with him," I explain, hoping he won't see him as a horrible person. Because as much as I know I don't want to be with him anymore, I don't want to brand him with that kind of label; it seems too much, too mean. Besides, some people can change and I hope that Ash is one of them.

"That's no excuse," she says. "If any of my boys ever spoke to a girl like he just did to you, they'd be in big trouble; I'd be so disappointed."

"You heard what he said?" I ask, becoming a little worried.

"He wasn't exactly quiet about it," she winces. "But you did the right thing and that's something to be proud of; that took a lot of guts! Now, your friends are outside, aren't they? Shall we go find them together, just in case he's lurking about outside?"

"That would be amazing, thank you," I say. As awkward as it is, I'm so grateful to have had her support through this. "What's your name, by the way?"

"Lydia," she says.

"Harper," I smile, reminded of how there are good people in the world too.

Lydia walks me out and it's easy to spot my friends hiding suspiciously (and very badly) behind some decorative bushes in the centre of the pavement.

"He's literally over there," Megan says, pointing down the street. I see the back of him as he walks further away; it might be the last time I ever see him again and I don't know how to feel about that yet. Relieved? Confused? Sad? I can figure that out later; I just need to keep telling myself that I only need to focus on one step at a time.

"It's okay," I say. "You can come out now, you know?"

They all walk towards us awkwardly, looking a tad embarrassed.

"It was a good idea at the time but hearing the way he spoke to you was awful," Zoe admits. "When we saw him storming out, we literally just fled."

"That sounds quite funny, actually," I say, trying to find another smile as I picture them all bolting frantically to hide from him.

"Well," Lydia says, clapping her hands together. "I'll leave you with your friends, but you know where we are if you ever need us."

"Thank you so much," I say again, hoping she can see how much I mean it. She walks back to the cafe and I turn to my friends. "And thanks to you guys for being there for me. That was really scary."

"But you did it!" Zoe says. "We're all really proud of you!"

"We never doubted you could," Kelsey says.

"Well..." Megan jokes, but honestly I think it would be valid; I didn't know if I could really go through with it until it was happening.

"What do you want to do now?" Zoe asks. That's a good question, actually. I can do anything I want and I don't have to run it by Ash first; I can simply be my own person again.

"Let's get ice-cream," I suggest.

"It's freezing!" Megan squeals,

"Yeah, but I have a craving!" I insist.

"Oh, well if it's a *craving*…" Megan groans comically. "Come on then, where's the best ice-cream place in this town?"

There's only one correct answer for this:

"It's down here," I say, and the four of us walk in the opposite direction to Ash, creating more distance between us. I try not to think about it too much because it's heavy and I still don't fully understand it all, but enough of me knows now that this is the best thing to do for myself. And I need to start doing things just for me more often; I will *never* let a boy take that away from me again. Well, I'll at least try and be a bit more aware of things like that; I don't think this is going to be a black and white learning curve at all.

***

When we arrive in the ice-cream parlour, I feel safer; it's like the walls are hugging me, protecting me from Ash who is outside. He's probably heading home right now, that's what I'd do in his situation. So, he's not coming; he won't even know I'm here at all because I've turned my location off.

And that makes me feel good.

Sad. But good.

"The menu is huge!" Megan exclaims after we slide into a booth. "How are we going to decide?"

"We could all get something different and then share?" Kelsey suggests.

"Yes, that's great! Are we all good with that?" Megan asks around the table. "Perfect, get picking, girlies!"

The distraction of choosing a flavour doesn't last long; as soon as I'm finished, my mind tries to wander back to Ash. I keep hoping he's okay and thinking about how he's feeling... if he's already at another girl's house. Those things shouldn't matter to me anymore, especially since he just proved again that he doesn't care if he hurts me, but they do. They might for a while, actually, and I'm not sure whether I need to try and suppress them or just accept it.

One step at a time, Harper.

I have to keep refocusing my thoughts on the here and now so it doesn't become too heavy.

And right now we are getting ice-cream.

"I am so excited," Zoe says. With our orders placed, we will only have to wait a few minutes and then I can just eat; eat and not think about everything else. I'm just a normal first-year student spending an afternoon with my friends and it doesn't matter in the slightest that I no longer have a boyfriend. It doesn't. It *really* doesn't.

Okay, so I don't think I'm ready for that yet; I'm still picturing him holding me close, stroking my hair as I listen to his heart-beat, and that is really not helpful.

It stings my stomach, making me sick to the thought of how I gave that up; I could have kept creating moments like that with Ash if I hadn't have broken up with him. But I also would have had to go through the other parts too, the darker ones. That's the important bit to remember; Ash wasn't capable of loving me well enough, but someone else will one day and I can't wait to meet them.

"That looks amazing!" Megan says, as a massive feast of a banana split is placed down in front of her. I don't think I've ever seen her eyes open so wide before.

One by one, we all receive our own orders and we begin taste-testing everything, dipping into each other's and chatting about normal teenage girl things. Kelsey even talks a little about Michael; while it hurts a little to hear how well they are doing after losing Ash, it does make me happy that he's good to her. It gives me hope that not all relationships are scary or dangerous; some are filled with security and fun.

"I am so glad you suggested ice-cream," Megan says with a mouthful of bubblegum. "I haven't had it in ages 'cos I was starting to think it was childish."

"I think it's good to do things you loved when you were younger," Zoe says. "You can connect with your inner child which is always nostalgic, but honestly, we just did some cool stuff when we were kids."

268

"Yeah, I had so much going on back then," I say; it's more of a reflection of how much everything has changed over the last year or so.

I came to uni because I wanted to learn more about the book industry so that I could write my own novels, but I've not written a single page of a story since being here. I do have a few plot ideas… It feels almost wrong to write about my experience with Ash, but literally every creative writing teacher I've ever had always says to write about what you know. And it feels right, you know? Like, I went through this horrible thing but I can turn it into something beautiful. I think there's something really powerful in that, something really strong. I won't be writing anything like that for a while so that I can get back on my feet, but who knows what will happen in a few months, how I'll be feeling?

"We should do this more often," Zoe says.

"This is the only good thing to come out of dating Ash," Megan adds jokingly.

"Well, he did bring a *few* more things to the table," I say, not quite ready to let those bits go yet.

"I can't wait for you to have a boyfriend who's actually grown up a bit. It's going to be amazing when it happens."

"Me too," I say, hopeful that we'll all find our person one day. I suppose it would have been all too convenient to have found my soulmate (if I even believe in all of that) the first time round. Maybe I'm supposed to find myself first before looking for someone else; that way I'll know who I am and what I want a lot more than I did when I was with Ash.

"Kels," Megan says. "You and Michael are setting the bar high; I hope you know that!"

"Oh, I'm *glad*," she says. "Boys like Ash need to realise they've got competition."

Boys like Ash. It feels wrong to say, like he's being labelled as a bad person and he can't change. I guess I have to be okay with knowing that this might be how it works out; he might never realise that how he treated Abbi and me was wrong. But I hope he does. I *really* do, because I want him to be happy and I don't think he can be while he's like this.

However, I also need to be happy; and that was becoming harder and harder the longer I stayed with him, waiting around for things to settle down when that might never happen.

And my friends? This little group of girls around the booth?

These people make me feel more loved than Ash ever did, and I know that as long as I have them, I can get through this.

270

Twenty Eight

After we finish up with our ice-creams, we head back to the train station. I'm so relieved to be putting more distance between Ash and I, mainly because I'm scared of what he means by 'this isn't finished'. That's also why I've been avoiding my phone, but to get my train ticket, I'm going to have to brave it.

As soon as I turn on the screen, my notification bar is filled with his name, each message somehow worse than the one before it.

harper.
come to mine so we can talk.

babe, please.

> you can't leave it like that. seriously, i don't want to keep asking.

> bitch.

Seeing the last one cuts the most; that one word is so harsh, so extra, so fake. It's hard to believe that I ever trusted him at all, or that I wanted to again once he came back. I can't lie, I do feel a little bit stupid, but I know why I did it; I was just trying to be the best girlfriend that I could be for him because I never want to be the bad guy. I don't want to ever give anyone a reason to hate me. Maybe I did with Ash without realising it, but I hope he won't feel that way forever.

I ignore the messages as well I can, purchasing and scanning my train ticket and spending most of the journey trying to laugh along with the girls. It's tricky but I did this before; I learned to live without having him around, so I know that I *can* do it again. I might not *want* to, but that's a different story; what I *want* doesn't matter anymore.

Not when I *need* peace.

We trudge back to campus, walking the same paths I've taken a hundred times before.

"Do you want to do anything today?" Zoe asks as we get back into the flat. All three girls are looking at me like it's completely up to me what we do and I feel overwhelmed at the fact I have to think coherently enough to make another decision. "We haven't eaten anything proper yet, do you want takeout?"

"Could we?" I ask, my eyes lighting up at the idea of a greasy pizza and fries.

"Of course we can, silly," she says. "Right, everyone head to my room and get the projector set up! I'm going to order our usual!"

"Thanks, Zoe," I say, so grateful for everything she's doing for me; I never made it easy for her. I wanted her to see the good in Ash so badly that I refused to listen to her warnings until it was too late.

"No problem," she smiles back and I follow Megan and Kelsey into Zoe's room. As usual, I feel comforted just by being in here; every time I've hung out with her in here, I've never had to worry about her shifting her mood, or hurting me in any way. I didn't realise it before. I took it for granted because I was blind to the fact that Ash has been manipulating everything all along to suit his needs, not caring who gets caught up in the fire. But I know now; I'm beginning to unravel it all and find my way back to who I want to be.

Megan begins to get the projector out from the drawer and balances it gently behind us on the bed frame. It's never been the greatest place to have it, but this is the only place we can put it so that it's facing a blank enough wall.

"What are we gonna watch?" she asks.

"Shouldn't we wait for Zoe to get back?" I ask.

"She will just tell you to pick," she says and, to be fair, she's probably right. "You want to watch *Dirty Dancing*? We know you *love* it!"

I think back to every time that Ash complained about it, telling me that it's only value was sexual. He missed the complete point of it all because he was only looking at it through his twisted little perspective; and that's how he always looked at me. I was only someone easy enough to bend and control, someone to have his way with until he got a little bit bored and jumped ship, until that ship sank and he swam right back to me. I'm not doing that again. I'm not falling for it.

And then I picture Nick and I sat in my room watching that same film; he *got* it. He understood all of it and I messed everything up because of my undying loyalty for someone who didn't actually have my back. Maybe choosing Nick wasn't necessarily the right option either, but it would have been better than running back to someone who left me.

"You know what, I'd love to watch it," I decide. This is me making a decision for myself, not clouding my thoughts with someone else's complaints.

"Fab," Megan says, searching for the disc by the pile of films. It's never too far down and she finds it easily enough. And just as she's setting it up, Zoe waltzes in.

274

"Won't be long!" she says, jumping onto the bed beside me.

And it really isn't; we're only about twenty minutes into the film when Kelsey and Zoe run out to go and get the takeout from the front door.

"You doing okay?" Megan asks me. It's weird seeing her so serious and calm but I'm not complaining.

"I think so," I say. "I'm more confused than anything, you know?"

"I'm not surprised," she sighs. "That was such a messy situation, but I'm glad you're out of it now."

"Me too," I say. "He's not completely bad, you know? He just has some things to work on."

"It's okay, Harper," she replies, giving me a pitiful look. "You're okay now."

I don't really know what she means by that since she avoided replying to me directly but how can I expect her to understand? She was never close to him in the way that I was; but I've seen all of him, every last inch of who he is and what I really hope he can be.

But no one will ever see him in the same way I will, not even Abbi, and I don't think I will ever change their minds. Because he may not be good for me now, but I really wish that he had been.

"It smells delicious!" Zoe exclaims as they come back, holding two pizza boxes, a large portion of chips and a massive bottle of Dr Pepper. We arrange it on the bed and snuggle up together to resume the film and, even though I know in my gut it's about to get a lot harder, for now, I'm okay.

I'm breathing. I'm smiling.

I'm reclaiming something small that he took from me. And it makes me realise just how much he took right in front of my eyes that I didn't notice before.

For the rest of the film, we laugh, we cry and we eat a lot of pizza. It's so comforting to know that no matter what happens with Ash, these three girls aren't going anywhere; maybe I've even made some friends for life.

But as the night creeps closer and the film ends, reality has to kick in a little.

"You gonna be okay tonight?" Zoe asks. Megan and Kelsey are looking at me too, almost as though they're scared of what I might say.

"I've done it before, haven't I?" I say, but my voice is wobbling a bit.

"You're doing really well," Zoe insists. "You got through the evening! I bet you didn't think you could do that."

"Yeah, I guess not," I say, taking a deep breath. "But I'll be okay. You guys need your sleep and we can't stay up all night."

"Are you sure?" Megan says.

"Yes, *please*," I reply. I don't want to ruin everyone else's sleep schedules along with mine. Actually, I don't want to ruin mine either; when Ash broke up with me before, I barely slept and it was awful. I was walking about like a zombie only when I needed the toilet or food, and my skin was so dehydrated that it had begun to peel a little. The thought of my body suffering again makes me feel sick and I make a small promise to myself that I will try as hard as I can to get through this in a healthier way.

"Okay, well, good night," Zoe says, bringing me in for a hug. "If you need any of us, you know where we are, okay?"

"Yeah, thank you," I say. "All of you. I really needed you today."

"We've always got your back," Kelsey says. "And Nick does too."

"I'm going to talk to him this week," I admit.

"Oh my god!" Megan says, suddenly getting excited.

"Not in that way," I say, calming her down. "I owe him an apology and an explanation. I treated him awfully because of how tunnel vision I was on Ash; I at least want to tell him that."

"That's really mature of you," Zoe says. "I'm sure he will appreciate it."

"I guess I'll have to let you know how it goes," I say. "Anyways, you should head to bed, guys. I'll speak to you all tomorrow, yeah?"

"Of course," Kelsey says. "Good night, Harper."

We all have a group hug in the middle of Zoe's room and I feel so enveloped in love that I hope I won't recognise the absence of Ash's.

Once I'm in my own bedroom and the door is closed behind me, I feel the silence I've been

277

dreading all evening. The hardest part of getting through times like these is the emptiness. That's what's dangerous, really, because it makes you want to reach out, ask them for a second chance, or maybe just even to talk. And that's what I'm thinking about as I get ready for bed and slide under the covers, remembering his scent behind me whenever he would hold me in this exact bed.

Now, it's just hollow.

Nothing more than a memory.

The darkness feels heavy too, like it's swallowing me up completely. And there's no one here to see my tears drip down softly onto my pillow, pooling on my sheets as I hold back my pain. It's too damn painful to cry entirely quietly; little moans escape here and there, highlighting every thought of Ash that passes through my mind.

And I hate it.

I hate how thinking about him brings me pain now and it's not even just about the fact that we're broken up. It's for all those things he shouldn't have ever done to me, all those things I thought were my fault and I deserved. It's for all those times I didn't stand up for myself, and for all those times where I gave in because he was my boyfriend and 'that's just what you do'.

It's for the girl who I was before him.

The girl I will probably never completely get back, because some part of me will always bear this tiny little scar, reminding me of what I went through. What I survived.

All I can hope is that the wound will heal over time, slowly fading until I won't feel any of this anymore.

Twenty Nine

Asking Nick if we can talk turns out a lot easier than how it went with Ash and I can't really be surprised, can I? He asks me straight away where I wants to meet up, and as soon as I suggest the hill on the outskirts of campus, he says that he will leave straight away. I am barely ready myself but I set off quickly enough.

I'm now walking across campus, clutching my phone like it's a lifeline and watching frantically for any sign of Ash prowling the streets watching out for me.

He said it 'wasn't finished', but since I ignored his messages last night, he hasn't tried anything else yet. So, as usual, he's being inconsistent. Damn, he's so obvious with it all; how blind was I? Still, I can't put it past him for him to turn up at my campus, stomping around and shouting about how I've 'embarrassed' him yet again.

"Hey," Nick says as I walk up to him. We're stood at the edge of the field, awkwardly in each other's presence. He looks so calm; his eyes seem kinder than before, if that's even possible. I really don't think that there's a single mean bone in his body.

"Hey," I reply. I'm not really sure what to do, but luckily he doesn't mind taking charge a bit; it's quite an admirable trait how brave he is socially. I wish I was like him in that sense. It would have made yesterday a lot easier.

"Do you want to go and sit at the top?" he looks behind him at the hill and I nod. The whole point of coming here was partly so that other people wouldn't be around to listen in, but I'm also starting to feel a little bit superstitious about coffee shops and cafes. I've had too many bad experiences in them this week and I don't want to add to that list.

We begin to climb the grass mound; it's easy at first but then the incline gets a little steeper. Reacting instantly, he holds out his hand to me and I take it gladly. The path that we've taken is a little muddy and I'm slipping about all over.

"Hopefully it will be a bit nicer at the top," I say.

"I brought a picnic blanket, just in case," he replies and I spot the bag on his back. I don't know how I missed it before, to be fair, but it doesn't matter; I'm justifiably distracted.

"That was probably a good idea," I laugh quietly. With his hand in mine, it's a lot easier to get through the rough patch and soon enough we've made it to the top. I love the view from here; you can see the whole campus and bits of the neighbouring town in the distance. It feels a world away from reality and everything that comes with it.

Most importantly, it feels far away from Ash.

Once we choose a good spot, he lays out the picnic blanket across the grass and we perch on it, sitting close but not touching, because I think even he knows that this isn't a date. There's probably not even a word for what this is; it's just two friends hanging out because one of them has to say sorry for being an absolute dunce.

"So," he says, looking at me. I'm shocked at the eye contact, but I can't drop mine now; he's committed so I have to as well. "What did you want to talk to me about?"

"It's not exactly an easy thing to say," I admit, twiddling my fingers in the bottom of my shirt.

"Don't worry," he comforts me. "Take your time."

"A lot has been going on this year," I begin. "We don't have forever so I can't explain all of it and I don't really *want* to either."

"Zoe told me a little bit. I hope that was okay?"

"Yeah, she said," I reply. "It's okay; it was probably for the best. At least Zoe was being a good friend while I couldn't be."

"You've *never* been a bad friend, Harper," he says, looking at me confused. "I didn't think that. Not ever."

"I have a bit," I say. "Last summer…" I breathe. This is the hard part: reliving it all. But he deserves it; if anyone needs an explanation, it's him. "Last summer, Ash and I got together. It was really good at first, or, at least, I thought it was. I'd never had a boyfriend before so I didn't really know how it's supposed to work. I still don't, I guess."

"That sounds tough," he replies.

"Yeah, it has been. But he broke up with me months ago… he was seeing another girl. I had my suspicions when we were still together but he just said I was being crazy, that I should just leave it alone because they were only friends. And then, somewhere down the line, he proved himself wrong."

"That's awful, Harper," Nick says. "I can't believe he could do that to you, just lie like it's nothing."

"After he left, I was practically rotting in my room," I continue. "I didn't know how I was going to get through it. And then I met you, and for a moment, it all felt okay again."

It feels weird to admit it, like it's wrong somehow. It makes it sound like I was just using him but that wasn't my intent at all; Nick, and whatever my feelings were for him, just came from nowhere.

"I didn't mean for any of it to happen," I explain. "I just got caught up in it… You made me happy."

"You made me happy too," he smiles. "But the timing was wrong, I know that."

"Yeah," I agree reluctantly. "When Ash came back after our date -"

"So, it *was* a date?" he laughs. "I knew it!"

"Ugh, fine, I guess it *was*!" I joke back. "But it threw me. He was saying everything I wanted to hear, painting it golden, and I believed it. I guess because I wanted to? I don't know, but he said that maybe we could try again."

"Maybe?"

"He was still with Abbi at this point," I say.

"Okay, that's a bit messed up," he comments.

"Yeah, it was," I admit. "But I wanted him back so much that I just didn't care about it as much as I should have, you know? And then I was in too deep; I thought that I couldn't get out and I had to make it work. I really wanted to fix it; but he didn't see anything wrong with us. So, I broke up with him yesterday and he got really angry - and - and he pushed me."

"How could he do that to you?" Nick questions, looking at me with such sincere eyes that I know he's not capable of treating me or anyone else like that. "Are you okay?"

"To be honest, I don't really know how to answer that," I say. "I'm still just trying to process everything; it may have been obvious to everyone else but it feels new to me, raw. It happened so quickly."

"That makes sense," he agrees. "You don't realise how bad it is until you leave, and then you keep looking back and noticing more and more things that were wrong too. It does get easier with time, though."

"How do you know?" I ask. I maybe shouldn't, it's rude to pry, but I can't help myself. The words just fall out and now I'm hanging onto his answer like it will solve everything.

"I had a similar experience with my first relationship," he says. "It was tough, but I can look back on it now and it doesn't hurt as much as it once did. And, honestly, I try to be grateful for it."

"What? Why would you do that?"

"Because it can't be undone, so why keep trying to make that happen? Why keep trying to forget? One day, I just decided to accept that it happened to me and learn from it; I used it to become a better person and to help other people."

"Like when you helped me at the pub?" I say, though it's not really a question. The memory just floats into my mind and I picture it all like it only just happened. It's scary to think about how much has changed since that night.

"Exactly," he says. "I used to have panic attacks all the time when I was with her. Either I didn't know what they were or I just didn't want to admit it, but they took over. No matter how many you have, each one feels like the first time all over again; you can't just convince yourself it's going to be fine when your brain and body is telling you the complete opposite on a loop. As soon as I noticed you were struggling, I knew I had to take you somewhere quieter, away from the crowd, and help you through it."

"It really helped," I say. "You, in general, really helped me get through this. But I guess that leads me to what I came here to say."

"I thought you just wanted to explain what happened? Why you've been MIA?"

"That was part of it," I say. "But I also wanted to say that I'm really sorry for leading you on. When I kissed you in the bar, I wasn't thinking about Ash. In fact, it was the first time in a long time that I wasn't. I was just really excited to be with you in that moment and I think that you and I get along really well."

"I think so too," he smiles softly.

"But that doesn't mean I think that we should get together or anything," I add in. His eyes squint a little but his face doesn't take long to relax.

"I understand that," he says. "We had really bad timing."

"Yeah," I reply. "Bad timing... I don't know if there would have been anything between us. Actually, no, I think there was *something*: a spark? But I'm not in a place to explore that right now; I have a lot of working on myself to do... a lot of moving on and making sure I'm okay."

"I get it, don't worry," he says. "We can just be friends. Though, I hope *good* friends?"

"Definitely!" I answer quickly. "I want you in my life, Nick. Just not in *that* way... right now."

"So, maybe one day?"

"I'm not saying wait around for me," I explain. "But we can just see what happens. I don't want to force anything or go into something too quick. But I'm not closed off forever."

"Forever is a long time..." he replies. "Hopefully it won't take you a lifetime to decide."

I laugh at him, shaking my head at how even in this difficult moment, he's still making me smile.

"I hope it doesn't! I don't want to give up on love entirely just because Ash wasn't the one," I decide. "I just want to hurt for a while; I want to understand what happened between me and him, and think about what I want for myself going forward."

"I think that's very mature," he says.

"Zoe said I was mature yesterday," I remember. "I guess I'm growing up?"

"That's what happens at uni," he says. "And a little heartbreak does give it a bit of a push too."

"I'll stick with the little bit," I laugh. "So, are we all good? You don't hate me or anything?"

"How many times do I have to tell you that I could never hate you?" he says, his eyes sparkling.

"Yeah, sorry…" I answer, feeling a little bit stupid.

"I'll tell you it as many times as you need. I'm here for you, Harper, friend or *girl*friend. And I'm not going anywhere."

He will never know how much those words mean to me, how important they are. No matter how horrible moving on from Ash is going to be, I need to remember that I'm not alone and I never have been; my friends will always be there to help me through things, just like I will be there for them.

Besides, I think there's something really beautiful in all of this: I'm about to find who Harper is by herself.

Epilogue

A few months later

"Wait, how long are you going for again?" Abbi asks as I put another shirt into my bag.

A few weeks after we had met at the coffee shop, I'd invited her if she wanted to meet up to talk about everything. I had to promise that it wasn't just so I could shout at her again and she agreed, thinking it a good idea to clear the air. And it definitely was; realising that she was never the enemy makes everything feel lighter, even if it was hard at first. But now she's part of the group and it makes me feel good... powerful... like Ash didn't break me completely.

"Literally just two nights," I remind her, trying to squeeze the zip shut.

"So why are you packing like you're going abroad for two weeks, then?" she laughs.

"I want choices!" I say. British weather is unpredictable at best but June just feels even riskier for some reason. Maybe it's because our expectations are higher; we want sun and warmth so we will most likely get drizzles and wind. "Besides, what if we end up going somewhere nice and I don't have something suitable?"

"He's not going to propose," Zoe mocks. "You guys aren't even together, remember?"

Ever since that day on the hill, when Nick and I spoke about everything, things have been different. The first few months were the hardest; I cried pretty much every night because I couldn't speak to Ash. He certainly tried, though. For a week or so, my phone was sporadically receiving nasty messages; he was even threatening to kill himself if I didn't answer. Those were the really hard ones to ignore. How was I supposed to know if he really meant it? That he might actually harm himself if I didn't give in? I couldn't know for certain.

But one day, they just stopped. I waited anxiously for them to come through again, for him to bang on my window in the middle of the night demanding to be let in. It was exhausting. He could have done anything and I would have had no power against him if I was by myself.

I've thought over these last few months about what I would do if I bumped into him and my answer changes every time. At first, I wasn't even going to go anywhere by myself, just to make sure I never fell into that situation. And then, once I started to feel a little better, I figured I'd at least say hi and see how he's doing. But now I just pray every day that I won't ever have to see him again. It hurt so much to move on but the important thing is that I did it. I may not be over what he *did* to me or how he treated me, but I don't think that I love him anymore. And I'm okay with that.

I doubt it would matter much anyway if we did see each other. It wasn't long after he stopped hounding me with messages that I realised the real reason why he gave up; it wasn't anything that I had done at all. He'd simply found someone else to drag along, to play the part of doting girlfriend while he gets off. And you know what, I wish her luck. I can't hate someone for replacing me, or for the fact that he's choosing *her*. Because at the end of the day, I just feel sorry for her. Hopefully, she won't be as weak as me and she will realise when his behaviour isn't acceptable, instead of painting all of the red flags until she's ready to leave.

But just because I'm over Ash doesn't mean that Nick is my boyfriend now, though I'm sure he'd love to be; I'm literally amazing. Seriously, though, we've just taken it slow and seen what we are like as friends. Luckily, we're really close and it's not as awkward as I was worried it might be. But he's been so understanding about where I'm at; I'm still not sure I'm ready to go into another relationship yet. I'm quite happy by myself, continuing to discover who I am and what I like and want from life.

It didn't stop him from inviting me to spend a weekend with him in London, though. He was so annoyed at Ash for ruining it for me that he practically insisted we do it properly, but I made him

291

wait until exams were over. I figured that was a valid enough reason to put it off for a while; the idea of going back made me uncomfortable for so long, tainted by memories I wish I didn't have. It's only been a few months, but I do feel ready to go back... to do it differently with someone new.

"Did you pack your toothbrush?" Kelsey asks, just as I have managed to finally close the zip. I look at her with a glazed expression.

"Meh, who needs to brush their teeth anyway?" I joke. "I'll go and get it. Wait, it's literally on my desk. I bought a new pack just for this trip.

"You're all flustered!" Zoe exclaims and my cheeks burn red.

"I am *not*!" I deny it, but I honestly think I am. It feels like this weekend could be really important, not just for me plastering over painful memories, but for making new ones with Nick... finding out if there is anything there between us. Or, maybe we are just destined to be really good friends. Oh, I don't know! But I'm excited to find out and I'm really glad that loving Ash didn't change my mindset about relationships permanently. Besides, Nick's promised me that we can sit in a coffee shop later this morning; he will be reading a book and I can have a bit of a writing session for the novel I started a while ago... I'm so excited to show him what I've been working on.

"Whatever you say," Zoe says, bringing me back to the present; she doesn't believe me for one second. But she's my best friend; being able to see right through me comes with the territory. "You better hurry up, though. Doesn't your train leave in like half an hour?"

"It's already half nine?!" I question in panic. I throw my Docs on, tying them as tightly as I can quickly, and then throw my bag over my shoulders. "Do I look okay? He's going to be here any minute!"

"You are so crushing on Nick," Megan smiles, shaking her head at how obvious I am.

"I'm not saying anything," I tease. "I just don't want to look like an idiot."

"You look amazing," Megan says, tucking my hair behind my ears so that it sits a bit nicer. "Who knows, maybe Nick will be doing that tonight when you guys decide to kiss," she adds with a knowing smile.

"We are *not* going to kiss," I blush. "We're just going to see London properly; do all the things I wanted to do last time."

Whenever I reference Ash and our relationship, the girls always tense up a little bit, unsure of how to react to me bringing it up. I think over time, as things got easier, they noticed that I was finding things okay again. They just want what's best for me and I am so grateful to have found that.

I had never really had a group of friends back home; I guess that's why I clung to Ash so tightly… once upon a time, he was all that I had.

But since coming to uni, I definitely got more than I ever expected and I wouldn't trade these

293

three for anything. Not even for him to come back, because all I ever wonder now is why I let all of that happen, why I let him return a second time and keep on hurting me. I won't be doing it again, whether it's with him or someone else, because I didn't deserve any of it.

No. I didn't at all.

But I see that now, even if it hurts to think about how someone could treat me like that, like I'm nothing.

And then someone is knocking on the door.

"Oh my gosh, it's him!" I squeal. "Hopefully he didn't hear any of that," I add in a more serious tone.

"Or the relationship could be over before it even started!" Abbi laughs.

"Do you want me to throw a pillow at you?" I joke.

"No, I want you to go and meet Nick at the bloody door!" she mocks back and I smile, thinking about how amazing this weekend is going to be.

"Right, I'm off!" We all clamber into the hallway and I lock my room behind us, enveloping them all in a hug. "I'll see you all on Sunday, and *yes*, I will give you *all* the juicy details!"

"We expected nothing less," Megan tuts. "See you later!"

I turn from them all and head to the front door. I know he's on the other side of it, waiting patiently for me, ready to take me to do something that's important to me... something I've wanted to do for years. And when I open it up, he's standing there.

Looking at me like I'm gold dust.

"Hello you," he says with a soft grin.

"Hey right back."

And there's no way I'm not blushing now.

Dear diary,

So much has happened this year that it's kind of hard to believe; it's like whiplash almost!

Starting uni was tough, especially when it took me away from Ash...

I guess that's another thing I should update you on. We did get back together temporarily but it felt so different; I didn't trust him at all. All I could think about was what he'd done with Abbi while we were together and it honestly just made me feel so rubbish about myself.

The good thing that came out of all of this mess is that I started therapy a few weeks ago. I've only had three sessions so far but it's really helpful to talk about everything that happened with someone. I feel seen. It also is making it clearer to me that I was never the issue when it came to our relationship; Ash was just not a good person... he might be one day but I don't have to wait around for that.

In the meantime, I've enjoyed being single and finding more love for myself, as well as time for my friends. The girls are an absolute laugh and Michael is surprisingly quite funny.

And Nick? Well, Nick and I are close. He's been so supportive throughout all of this that I feel really lucky to have him around.

Well, that's all the updates for now! For now, London awaits! ♡

Harper

Acknowledgements

It is a very surreal feeling to be writing the acknowledgements for this book. It has been an idea in my head for so many years that I had almost accepted that it would never become anything. Yet, here we are... at the end, or is it just the beginning? Either way, now is the time to send my thanks out into the world!

Firstly, thank you to Emma Smith. Other than the fact your books are a huge inspiration to me, you have given so much of your time and dedication into producing the most wonderful cover and graphics. I'm also extremely grateful for all of your advice throughout the process and for being my first beta reader.

Secondly, I'd like to shout out my amazing friend of many years, George Somers, for her beautiful poem at the beginning of this book. It feels really special, after all this time, to be able to use it. I feel extremely lucky to be in your life and I cannot wait to support you and your future work.

Next, thank you to my family, friends and boyfriend for always sticking by me. I can be incredibly introverted, clicking away at my keyboard, but I know you all recognise how much I love writing.

And lastly, thank you to everyone who has supported me on social media and my books, especially those of you that have become close friends over the last few months. You don't have the slightest idea how much I appreciate the support you all give and I hope from the bottom of my heart that you enjoyed *Lost For You*. I certainly enjoyed writing it, though it was definitely emotional at times. However, I found comfort between its pages and I wish the same for you.

~ Faith

faith fawcett

Faith has always been an avid reader with a love for writing. Her favourite memories are those moments when she was tucked up in bed with characters like Anne of Green Gables and Hetty Feather!

books for children:

books for young adults:

Faith Fawcett Author on Facebook
@faith3699 on TikTok
@_faith_fawcett_author on Instagram

Printed in Great Britain
by Amazon